THE LEGEND OF LIZ AND JOE

THE LEGEND OF LIZ AND JOE

John Murray

FlambardPress

First published in Great Britain in 2009 by Flambard Press
16 Black Swan Court, 69 Westgate Road, Newcastle upon Tyne NE1 1SG
www.flambardpress.co.uk

Typeset by BookType
Cover artwork © Andrew Foley
Design by Gainford Design Associates
Printed in Great Britain by Cromwell Press Group, Trowbridge, Wiltshire

A CIP catalogue record for this book is available from the British Library.

ISBN: 9781906601072

Flambard Press wishes to thank Arts Council England
for its financial support.

Flambard Press is a member of Inpress.

The paper used for this book is FSC accredited.

For Annie and Ione, with lots of love

Also love and special thanks to Bonnie

(from 'Twelve Sidelong Glances')

'9. Alternatives . . .

d) Exasperate their biases. This would be the contrary tendency. At any given moment in any given domain only one thing would be in fashion: basketball boots, for example, or chili con carne, or Bruckner's symphonies. Then it would change: sewerman's boots, tarte Tatin, Corelli's church sonatas. To lend the whole thing greater weight (and enable the leaders of our country to stand up more effectively to the economic crises they have to confront), one might assume that these imperatives had the force of law. The population would be warned in good time via the press of the conditions under which they would henceforth be required to be shod, to eat and to listen to music.'

> Georges Perec, *Species of Spaces and Other Pieces*
> (translated by John Sturrock)

'Then he crawled farther back from the gap and taking off his braces altogether made it into a belt. It hurt his hips, but he felt far better and manly.'

> Liam O'Flaherty, *Three Lambs*

'"What a night!" said Marthe, "And then what do you think we are, you and I, at our age!"
"We are alive," said Jourdan.'

> Jean Giono, *Joy of Man's Desiring*
> (translated by Katherine Allen Clarke)

1

Three Memos to Self, 5 December 2008

1.

In today's local paper there is a letter from an apparent
lunatic ranting about the contemporary scourge of the grey
squirrel and its routing of the native red variety hereabouts.
Let's keep this lethal foreign pest out of our precious
Cumbrian countryside, and by all means necessary pre-
serve our native species! the gentleman correspondent
urges with a frothy forthrightness that would have impressed some of those who once made star appearances
at Nuremberg. And yes, to be sure, I know all about the
rampant grey squirrel pox which some say kills off all the
reds and not the greys . . . but I am also old enough to
remember when some of the shooting estates paid a
bounty for the tails of slaughtered red squirrels. They were
supposed to eat game bird eggs you see, which meant that
anything could be done to them and by all means necessary. Once it was the demon reds and now it is the demon
greys, and be assured that some of those slavering country-
men will only be happy when they have potshotted more
or less everything that moves.

On the same day in the national paper a cabinet minister
broaches the possibility of an affirmative British citizenship
test, not to be applied to off-colour squirrels, I think I'm
right in saying, but to humans who might possibly be
regarded as off-colour and especially if they happen to be
foreign. It would seem that immigrant Somalis, Estonians,

Bulgarians, Bangladeshis etc. who wish to share our fabled bounty and experience our long-lauded bulldog courtesy and generosity will need to learn by rote a few Hanoverian lineages, a few essential patriotic facts relating to Great Men who happened to be admirals, generals, architects, colonial administrators. They might also be subject to a spot check to see if they know the precise and undistorted lyrics of the National Anthem and be obliged to sing it fortissimo in the street or be booted out of the country forthwith.

It is truly beyond parody all of this, this miserly grudgingness here in Albion in 2008, and it has set my old mind thinking . . .

2.

I'm also thinking of doing a Greek banquet tomorrow night in The Lonning. It occurs to me if the combination of okra with figs works, as it most certainly does, then experimenting with okra and fresh apricots might also produce a sublime supplementary dish. The recipe for *bamies me seeka* was given to me by volatile but generous old Manolis when Liz and I were staying in Sikinos back in the Seventies. Manolis drank like a fish in the Alopronia taverna though to be honest all three of us did once we got started, the retsina tasted so pungent and fine and the little island was so lovely and in those days was barely visited by foreigners. Manolis wore a stiff and smart maritime cap even though he was never a sailor; it was only his fisherman's tribute to the majesty of the sea as it were. He said he got the *bamies me seeka* recipe from his aunt who came from remote unvisited Kithnos and she in turn had got it from a ship's cook who hailed from a tiny village in the far west of Crete. Doubtless the cook got it from his long dead Cretan grandmother whose own grandmother lived under Ottoman rule, so we will never know where the recipe really started nor who has proprietorial rights

10

on it. The same, it occurs to me applies to words as well as recipes, and these are two of the things that frequently occupy my imagination. It is an absurd reflection, but someone somewhere must have been the very first person to use such and such a word in any given language, it came from a human throat, not from the rocks or the skies or the wordless ocean. Likewise someone somewhere in our own dear land was once the very first to utter the words rhubarb, iced bun, egg, hornbill, lampoon, persiflage, fart, Clarence, costive, cummerbund . . .

3.

Blackbird is a 2 that is 1. Teaspoon is a 2 for stirring 1. Beanbag is a 2 full of 1. Whitethroat is an ext. that has a 2 that is 1. Knowall is an ext. who 1's 2. Moneybags is an ext. who has 2 of 1. What is unarguable is that we immediately understand the precise semantic relationships of binary compound words without having to think about them. We don't for example think a teaspoon is a spoon made out of tea, or that a beanbag is a bag for storing kidney beans in, or that a moneybags is a quantity of bags for keeping money in. Possibly I suppose in cases of severe autism or in certain neurological conditions, they don't understand the inner connections of compound words, and it causes unforeseen consequences at times? On that interesting line of thought, take the instructive case of dogmeat, which is a 2 for 1, and catmeat that is also 2 for 1, and then, with a shudder, take horsemeat that is a 2 *of* 1. We don't as a rule shudder at the words dogmeat and catmeat, but we do, unless we are certain unsqueamish French or Belgian carnivores, flinch at the word horsemeat, and none of us even for a split second thinks that it is meat that we feed to a horse. Extrapolating laterally, I don't know any Korean or Tagalog, but I imagine that in Korea and the Philippines where some of the citizens eat dog, they must have two separate compound words for the dogmeat that is 2 *for* 1 and for the dogmeat that is 2 *of* 1.

Or it could linguistically be entirely otherwise, and perhaps they never use binary words in such cases. After all the English word 'veal' exists, but not 'calfmeat', though in my case as a strict vegetarian both of those designations make me feel profoundly sick at the very idea . . .

As I said, Memo Number 1 set my old mind thinking . . .

Look (*lookster!*). About this controversial pilot scheme? Were we properly 'braced' for the new legislation?

That sweltering week in the late summer of 2017 (*when wi wuss aw swettin greet cobs as big as hummin bummlies*) there was a surprise announcement from the government, which had the whole of our customarily imperturbable county of Cumbria dumbfounded (*sister, yan er tyan ev us vanya tyan a bliddy hearty tack!*). Once again it had been singled out (*wi got pickt on, let's fyass it, like wi allus git bliddy pickt on*) for a significant national pilot role, a testing ground for an important social experiment, although in this case instead of advancing and toe-dipping the digital age, it was something of a more inscrutable item of socio-cultural research (*a sowshal wassacomie hartyfarty sek an sek*).

Whoops. My apologies. Let me swiftly put you in the picture re the above, which happens to be the first paragraph of a very important project I am working on . . .

Last year a London-based businessman, a food manu-facturing magnate drunk on the meteoric success of his national sales, and the massive state-of-the-art factory he had recently had built in West Cumbria, had decided to express his gratitude to the host county in as fitting a manner as possible. His largesse took the form of offering a generous prize for the best unpublished story (comic tall tale preferred) or play (preferably a lighthearted farce) or collection of poems (humorous verse ideally) in the good old Cumbrian dialect, something unremarkable enough given the prominence and longevity of the local dialect societies and the regular festivals and competitive performances in various villages and coastal towns year in year out. Unremarkable that is, were it not for the fact that instead of offering a trophy or a tankard or a hundred pounds worth of his unbeatable sausages and pies for the most ventriloquial verbal dialect feat, he was offering a *fifty thousand pounds* cheque for an original work of dialect literature.

'Bloody hell,' said half of Cumbria, and the other half gasped, *'Fuck me gently an hoo the ell is ah spost ter write it aw doon ter impress a bliddy Lunnon tykoon?'*

That wasn't the only surprise. There were to be no runners-up, the magnate solemnly insisted, and no consolation prizes, just one dialect genius who was to collar the lot. By this one took it perhaps to signify that he himself had no real competitors or runners-up, either inside or outside the county, though plenty of also-rans in all four quarters of the globe when it came to processed food manufacture. He needed a judging system of course, which was where his maverick prodigality suddenly took on a worried look. This might just have been because by all accounts he claimed only to really understand the dialect himself when he was drunk. He did some hurried consultation and eventually chose a predictable two or three 'experts', comprising an affable Border TV personality whose grasp of the dialect nuances I anticipated would be as convincing as his gurgling enthusiasm for our quaint regional customs; a former local journalist of mature years and fondness for the bottle who paradoxically might not be altogether hopeless at sorting out the dialect shit from the dialect sugar . . . and an actual dialect practitioner whose face fell at the fait accompli press announcement naming him for definite and without consultation as one of the judges. It meant of course he could not compete for the fifty grand himself, and no doubt all sorts of pained and hostile judging principles suddenly came to mind (the winner must be over sixty-five, stone deaf and/or severely myopic and have ten generations of dialect-speaking fore-bears who had *never once* left the same ancestral village) when he thought of some fly-by-night buffoon or even worse one of his doughty old dialect personality competitors swooping down like an eagle and bearing away that colossal amount of cash.

Before I continue with the draft of my entry to the competition, let me point out what might not be obvious at all. My original composition, which I earnestly hope will hoover up the fifty grand after ten minutes take-it-as-read deliberation by the assembled judges, is written entirely in echt and flawless Cumbrian dialect – albeit with my own impertinent phonetic and punning distortion. I am after all supposed to be writing a tale that is not only tall but comic. Because no one outside the county, or for that matter about sixty per cent within it, would be able to grasp what I have written in all its depth and width and breadth etc., I am obliged to give you a version in an imaginative but I promise you accurate and undistorted translation. To be precise, the translation is not word for word literal, but sense unit for sense unit literal. Meaning I have had the considerable task of conveying the unique comic nuances of the sounds and syntax of the extraordinary hybrid and archaic Nordic language which is contemporary Cumbrian dialect. As a direct consequence, you understand, of successive waves of Viking invasion into ancient Cumbria, the region became and has since remained linguistically heavily Scandinavian . . . and though we are not actually called Knut or Gudrun or Ulf round here, inside us lurking are so many simulacral ancestral Knuts and Gudruns and Ulfs . . . believe you me.

So it is that my translation includes selective extracts from the dialect original, the latter being embedded and bracketed at appropriate points, as a constant reminder of the source from which the translation came. I did as it happens briefly think of making complete and separate dialect and English versions, and even of putting them side by side on opposing pages, but on reflection realised that all that would achieve would be to give you a chronic squint, and put you off the versatile charms of the dialect literature for evermore.

Continuation of dialect story *Galluses Galore*

A decade earlier, back in 2007, the peaceable and innocuous West Cumbrian port of Whitehaven (*slippy owd snurrin owd Whitehebben*) had been specially chosen as the very first guinea-pig place in the country to have its analogue television signal removed. Henceforth (*hen's fyeut*) all Whitehaven goggle boxes were to be functional only in a kaleidoscopic digital profusion (*wi thi hanset like a funny laal wocky tocky jammt in thi hant, thoo can click an punsh awae an niffer be bored ter deeth ivver agyan*). We were talking, were we not, about changing from a niggardly five channels to a sumptuous and expansive five hundred, and that we should stress was only to mention the good old telly. As for the digital radio, that could also be 'viewed' by riveting magic through the blank TV screen (*grantit neah HD piksher, but plenny ev luffly wassacomie DABBY DAB soont*). It would offer any dish-owning Copelanders everything from Punjabi folk music to Christian evangelical broadcasts to diseases in fish-farming documentaries from Radio nan Gaidheal, to vintage archival Pink Floyd (*t'langhairt drug-swallerin marraboys wat singed aboot climmin an fleein roont T' Wo*) on BBC 6, to vintage Milton in the form of *Paradise Lost* in two hundred fifteen-minute episodes on BBC 7. In response to the long announced government injunction, digiboxes and satellite dishes obediently began to sprout in the Copeland capital like rampant daisies or stinkworts (*like seah many bliddy owd stingwoords*), while for example in the nearby amiably competitive township of Workington (*t' fenerable but envyus cappytal ev Halledyal*) the trapped-in-a-time-warp Wyrkentonians were still footling away with their miserly old five terrestrials.

But this new and radical 2017 legislation which was relayed via the local government HQs in Carlisle, Eden, Copeland, Allerdale, Kendal and Barrow-in Furness . . . was more than just another example of compulsory substitution or replacement (*when t'guffment gadgers sez stop dyeuhin yah thing an start dyeuhin t' udder*). The principal difference was that instead of the new replacing the old, as with the handsome satellite dish replacing the idiotic pronged tuning fork-aerial on all those thousands of Whitehaven walls, roofs and gable ends . . . this was a case of the picturesque old replacing the vulgar new. Moreover, instead of being something relatively intelligible, viz. digital TV advancement (*dishy tall 'aw stashuns go', marra!*) equals associated information technology advancement . . . meaning not just local but national, hence transnational, hence multinational, hence supranational economic advancement . . . the reasoning behind this other pilot legislation was a touch obscure. After all, it might end in the sound 'shun' like information does, but specialised *fashion*, and specialised male fashion at that, seemed an extraordinarily unversatile and unexploitable entity to test out even on the meek and docile citizenry of Cumbria. And by this we are not talking about trying it out on a single town like Whitehaven, but about experimenting on pan-Cumbria (*on pan bliddy Cummerlan!*), or at any rate we are talking about what was to seriously affect every single Cumbrian adult male . . .

This is what happened:

Thomas Purley, our government premier (*t' top gadger, Tommy Pullet. Him wat cem efter t'marraboy wat cem efter Cotton Bruin, wat cem efter Tant Blur, wat cem after a lang line ev varra strang an carrysmackit lidders wat startit wit owd Madgie Thunder the fair-hairt but gey tyeuf-talkin Torry*) had been lying awake many a night puzzling over what it was he saw as a quintessential loss or lack of something in the British constitution. Which is to say, he was worrying himself quite sick about the state of the British character rather than the statutory laws of the land or anything like that. Wherever one looked these days in 2017 in the UK one saw painful (*aw dirry me*) evidence of antisocial and truculent behaviour (*fandals, tykes an bliddy warlicks*): in schools, factories, football crowds and pitches, shopping malls most obviously, but also and sadly even in small rural towns, in the countryside itself (*bad gets ev country warlicks wat gits full ev yal an sighter, an gabs on t'bliddy rampish even in t'bliddy pissable owd countryside*), in the shires, in what had once been the Tory heartland (*Sir Horris, Sir Harrel, Leddy Sek and Sek, Dame Wassname ant Rite Horrible Gadger This, an Rite Ellish Gadger That*) and where the enduring and, one might have fondly hoped, unassailable and unfathomable and sacred and more or less mystical tear-inducing moiety known as 'Britishness' might have been said to be invulnerable.

The said premier (*t'syam top gadger*) had been lying awake night after night that long and roasting summer, trying to think of some comprehensive solution, some skilful social remedy to mitigate this ambient moral decay which was alas (*dirry dirry me*) most painfully conspicuous amongst today's male youth. We all know about hoods, of course, and we are not talking about the monastic variety.

17

Hoods on male youngsters in urban shopping malls, meaning repugnant indices of sloth, defiance, deception . . . and hump-backed unforward-looking unmanly slouching! The police knew well enough to focus on the hooded before focusing on the hoodless, but what other totemic items of fashion which blatantly stood for surly non-conformity, anti-Britishness, not pulling together as a team etc., might it be possible to proscribe? Suddenly, lying bone awake that night and tossing in his overheated bed, the premier (*t'top gadger*) was visited by an ancient and very vivid memory which seemed to him to attest to the power not only of the precious values that were sadly gone, but also to the charismatic power (*carry smackit poor*) of parental instruction, parental guidelines, parental values, in a word parental morality.

Purley was thinking back to 1961 which also had a roasting summer and when the Tories were impregnably in power. The premier (*t'top gadger*) was then only ten years old (*an ee ed shot back and sights, greet sticky oot lugs, an a flaysome owd catpullet hinging oot his britches pockit*) when one Sunday morning he had been fiercely upbraided by his dear old mother. Then in her sober and testy mid-forties and of sternly respectable working-class Tory-voting origin, she had suddenly taken one look at his dirty knees and general dishevelment, his hair sticking up all over the place just like something out of *Just William* (*Rishmal Cumpton body's 'Chuss Willum'*) and felt an angry sinking of the parental heart.

'You!' she cried. 'I will not have it!'

Thinking perhaps she was accusing their mischievous dog Winston of some characteristic heinous crime, the startled premier (*t'top gadger*) in miniature (*in laal facksimly portytype*) looked behind him and squeaked anxiously: 'Not have what, Mum?'

'That!' she cried, pointing not at Winston who was out roaming in the back garden but at the waist of her little son. 'That horrible, vulgar, common, coarse contraption you have on you!'

Her son looked down baffled at his waist and could see nothing apart from his unbuttoned shirt and his innocently peeping belly button.

'That *belt*!' she snorted. 'That common vulgar belt you have around your waist. Even worse, it's a snake belt isn't it? Which means it makes me seriously ill to look at it.'

Her son had no choice but to concur. It was indeed a striped fabric snake belt where the hook at the end went into the metal ring, a snake cheerfully holding its own tail as it were. They were all the rage in 1961 among ten-year-old boys and even the future premier (*t'top gadger stannin in t'wings seah ter say*) was capable of being bowled over by a common pre-pubertal craze.

Her son could have asked her what was so vulgar, common and bilious-looking about a little fabric snake belt, but he didn't. Even then, as a wide-eyed young sprout, he knew that the parental instincts were the right ones and this thing about his waist was thenceforth truly vulgar and abhorrent. He was about to remove it without further demur when his mother anxiously cried: 'No! Don't remove it yet, Thomas!'

'No?' exclaimed her flummoxed offspring.

'If you do, your trousers will fall down, and that'll be no solution. But look, here's ten shillings. Go and get the bus into town and when you get there go to Timmits and buy yourself a nice new pair of *braces*.'

Braces? Even docile young Thomas felt his face fall at that. He echoed the incredible word: 'Bra–'

'Yes, good old braces. Good old, good old, good old braces (*guid owd gallusish*)! They are plain, simple, well-meaning, innocent, respectable and you can hang all your best principles on them. They are not like snake belts . . . not like sly, creeping, untrustworthy and horrible slithering snakes. They are good, old fashioned, and they represent a really lovely bygone age (*a mashless yootoopey frae lang sen*).'

To cut a long story short the premier (*t'top gadger*) in 1961 had had a 'braces conversion', and in replacing his cheap and tawdry transatlantic little belt with some pious and humble and infinitely British braces, he knew himself to once again be at one with the world or at any rate back in his darling mother's tender graces (*an tek speshul nowt that 'bressis' an 'gressis' byath rime*). By doing nothing more troublesome in 1961 than changing an unseemly fashion for a seemly one he had somehow restored cherished principles and personal discipline, and it left him feeling virtuously and justly euphoric.

So it was that more than half a century later, in 2017, he knew that he could affect a similar conversion upon the country that he ruled, and he at once set in motion the ground-breaking compulsory braces legislation, meaning the Obligatory Braces Act 2017, which was to be the one piece of Thomas Purley's social strategy (*Tommy Pullet's yah lezhndry bit ev sowshal henshineerin*) that was to be mulled over and analysed by future historians more than any other.

At first and reasonably enough Premier Purley intended his radical edict to be enacted nationwide, but after consultation with his most trusted ministers, he agreed to an initial toe-dipping pilot scheme. A sample geographical area was mooted and the beaming young Transport Minister said: 'I think it should start with a C and end with an A, this sample area!'

After protracted, not to say puzzled, meditation the premier asked, 'Canada?'

'Not at all, Tom. That's only a dull sort of Dominion. That's not really us in the best sense.'

'An area which when no one is listening we like to call "Caca"?' chortled the deputy premier (*t'vanya top gadger*). 'Meaning Inner City London? Belfast? British Honduras?'

'No, no, I mean Cumbria of course (*Cummerlan ev cworse*). It's the only pilot area we have that's been set aside as purpose-built for experiments of all kinds. Remember Calder Hall (*can thoo aw mind Call A Halt*)? Remember Sellafield (*can thoo mind sek as Sellerfell as weel*)? Remember all those Cumbrian POW camps (*can thoo mind aw them vankisht Joormans, Eyeties, Nastys an Fushishtsh*) after the last war?'

'No,' said the premier (*t'top gadger*). 'But I do remember a scout trip up to Buttermere back in 1963. And it rained and rained and rained and wouldn't damn well stop (*it pisht an pisht and pisht, and yance it ed stoppt it decidit it wantit ter start up agyan*). Since then I've always somehow felt in at least two minds about the place.'

To leave off this incontinent however impassioned political dialogue and resume the pungent narrative. As of 21st December 2017 every single adult male Cumbrian was legally required to wear braces to keep up his trousers, and could face a heavy fine or ultimately a robust prison sentence if he persistently refused to do so (*Haffrig if thoo's lucky, an Durram if thoo isn't*). Henceforth neither leather nor plastic nor any other kind of belts would be permitted around the male Cumbrian waist, nor for that matter would the option of nothing save gravity and one's belly and embonpoint and jutting backside to hold up one's trousers be countenanced as a feasible alternative! From now on one could not legally wear a belt, but neither could one legally wear nothing! It was braces or bust, you understand, here in pilot scheme Cumbria from Christmas 2017 onwards.

End of instalment of *Galluses Galore*

The author of the above, also of course your narrator, is called Joe Gladstone, and he is now going to tell you about his wife and his business and his supposedly unusual and exacting take on life. At a suitable juncture he will then return to the dialect tale about compulsory galluses, and at a second suitable juncture he will then tell you more about himself and Liz and the paradise called The Lonning, and the best way to cook zucchini and about compound words and about the authentic power as opposed to the sentimental quaintness of the dialect. You will be pleased to know: 1) That he will stop talking about himself in the third person at this point and, 2) That this amiable and alternating progression I have just described will not, I promise, go on like the Sargasso Sea ad infinitum.

To begin with one or two crucial first principles. My wife, God bless her, thinks that I am something of an all-round idiot, but really she doesn't know the half of it. For a start she doesn't have the faintest clue about what really goes on inside my cantankerous head, just as I have no firm idea of what really goes on inside that ever vigilant scope of hers. In my own case, and to flatter myself, I mean what I think of as the inscrutable ruminative pauses, the faintly perceived yet luminous and numinous inner spaces, the things I can only think of as inarticulable imaginative lacunae, the unsayable intimations of all sorts of things profound and unprofound, the hints neither broad nor narrow, the thoughts that are neither words nor not words, and so on and so forth. In my wife's case, I have even less authoritative notion of the warp and weft of her subtlest inner life, now that she is having experiences which would seem to be beyond both our kens. Of these remarkable experiences, more later, but just to hint that their arrival in her old age would seem more appropriate than for her to have experienced them in her teens. They are of a nature unarguably beyond the empirical, the mundane, the normal, which I stoutly insist is not the same as that cooked up, spurious and conflatory term the 'paranormal'.

Elizabeth, aka Liz, is seventy-three, and I am also seventy-three. She is thin and beautiful and provident, and I am thin, not outstandingly ugly, but impulsive and at times impossible. I have always been spendthrift and impractical, but once I turned seventy I was briefly stinking rich, and without having struck a bat as it were to achieve these riches. What happened was my Uncle Harrison, a restless hard-working hill farmer, died three years ago in his mid-eighties, having left me his beautiful North Cumbrian smallholding tucked away in these obscure north-east uplands. The farmhouse and outbuildings are seventeenth century and at the end of a narrow D-Road, which is sporadically tarmacked by the county council but nevertheless has vigorous weeds sprouting through it just as if it was a highway in the remotest Outer Hebrides.

My uncle was what people would call a character, a meaningless designation if ever there was, as what some people would class as a character I would class as a person wholly lacking one. Harrison was born in 1920 and died in 2005, a day or two before his favourite nephew Joe turned seventy. He was a loud and volatile and optimistic bachelor with a bristling almost electrical moustache, big and hairy ears, idiosyncratic but sympathetic looks, and a prize herd of Charolais cattle. He had inherited The Lonning from his father, my great-uncle Willy, a bad-tempered misunderstood man who used more foaming expletives per sentences than anyone I have ever met. Son Harrison's passions were English and Scottish hound trails, horse racing, beer drinking, dominoes, smart and expensive shoes, meaning the handsomest and most costly brogues, boots, suedes, slip-ons and latterly amazingly Nike bloody trainers, he could unearth from the shoeshops both sides of the Border in Carlisle, Brampton, Annan, Dumfries and even Hawick in Roxburghshire, if he could be bothered to drive that far.

Harrison was also an expert at leek growing, an addict of leek-club competitions both Cumbrian and Northumbrian, and ditto of onion growing and onion competitions. He grew leeks the length of a gladiolus and the width of a barometer, vegetables that were quite inedible of course, they were of such a freakish and mutated constitution. Why size in the competitive horticultural world should mean greatness is more or less beyond me, the only symbolic parallel being that of the grower's genital dimensions, as I suppose most leek growers are males and some of them without a word of a lie would burgle, sabotage, possibly maim and disable their fellow competitors if it meant they could win a first prize at their respective Leek Clubs.

When Harrison died he left everything to me, including The Lonning with all its irreplaceable antique contents, and his savings of about three quarters of a million pounds. Of course few seventy-year-olds receive such enormous bequests, but as far as Harrison was concerned I was only a bit of a wet-around-the-lugs bairn at three score and ten. Liz was both amazed and delighted, because now that she was seventy she could optionally throw in her workaholic business as an interior designer and live in amiable please-herself retirement. She had earned the bulk of our income for the forty-five years of our marriage, while I had made what I could out of my cookery books. One of them on gourmet vegetarian cuisine published when I was sixty had briefly been a bestseller and then as swiftly remaindered by a sadistic, probably drunken publishing decision I never understood. At this point I can say objectively, impersonally, and as if I talking about someone else's book rather than my own, that it is one of the finest cookery books ever written in any language, but that makes no damn difference when it comes to the deplorable public taste (and yes the pun is deliberate). They, the idiotic public, buy books by buffoonish TV chefs, those that have telly tie-ins, and give them to each other for Christmas, make two dog's dinners of the most boring recipes on Boxing Day and 27 December respectively, and then beamingly slap them away on their veneer bookshelves and leave them there untouched for evermore.

Harrison's legacy put paid to the ignominy of that, thank God, even if only temporarily. No more need I publish brilliant cookbooks that only a handful of serious cooks would ever take seriously. There and then I decided I would turn The Lonning into not a gourmet restaurant, but a *gourmet guest house*, and I would use a good bit of the three quarters of a million to refurbish it in the style to which my gourmet food would wish to be accustomed. To Liz's fury, I was not going to charge an arm and a leg for people to stay in the guest house where the cost would include the exquisite evening meals whether said guests wanted them or not. My tariffs would be reasonable, almost too damn reasonable, when it came to making anything as down to earth and banal as a commercial profit. The quirk, the hitch, the paradox was that although in relative terms my guest house would be dirt cheap, entrance to it would be got at, how shall I put it?, at a certain personal cost . . .

To be sure I am not talking about the Third World potholes and weedy tarmac, the closed gates on the road that signify the demarcations between successive remote farms, or my neighbour Tommy's dawdling cows which like to ruminate at their leisure upon whatever greenstuff sprouts beside the road. All of this, needless to say, requires a certain stout patience on the part of any putative discerning tourist heading in my direction.

'You what?' said Liz, with stern suspicion in her voice when she heard me mention 'personal cost'. 'Meaning what exactly?'

'I am not,' I said defiantly, 'letting any old Tom, Dick and Harry into my hard-won gourmet guest house.'

'Pah. What do you mean, hard-won? A fortune dropped into your idle lap, just as things have always fallen into it, including myself, your far too supportive wife. As for riff-raff, I should hope not. No drunks, loudmouths, stag nights, hen nights, none of those buggers.'

'Take that as read, Liz,' I snorted. 'No what I mean is, I'm not letting any old bore or group of bores into The Lonning as guests, even if they brandish ten times the rate, even if they were to bribe me with priceless Scotch or nineteenth-century port. I want only extremely interesting people in my guest house.'

She sneered and possibly shuddered. 'Oh really? Bit of a tall order isn't it. What are you going to do, set them an IQ test in the hallway and/or demand they supply you with a Rorschach blot or two?'

I smirked triumphantly. 'Not far off. Very warm indeed as a matter of fact.'

She definitely shuddered then. 'You what, you certifiable crackpot?'

I was just about to describe to you in methodical and dogged blow-by-blow fashion, my foolproof patent method for keeping dreary people well clear of The Lonning Exclusive North Cumbrian Guest House. Instead of that I shall cut to the quick, take a handy narrative shortcut, and indicate as much in illustrative epistolary fashion. I do this because only this morning I had penned a rejection letter to one of those persistent would-be guests, who simply would not take no for an answer.

The Lonning
Mallstown
Cumbria

5 December 2008

Dear Mr Barkis,
I am so sorry to disappoint you yet again (*I almost began, Barkis, I ain't willin*). You have clearly strug-gled with commendable diligence to fit my some

might say outrageous requirements, but sad to say I still don't feel in my heart of hearts that you are what I would candidly regard as an interesting individual. In part I feel a certain pity on your behalf, as you seem to want to sample my legendary food and stay a few nights in my lovely guesthouse with a quite extraordinary persistence. Over the years you say you have read the two or three write-ups in the weekend colour supps and have been attracted no doubt by its fabled exclusivity. You were, you add, rather stunned by the fact I have always refused to allow any of the colour supp journalists to come and sample my cuisine and my hospitality firsthand. The grounds for this, as you might imagine, were that they themselves had to submit to my standard short-essay require-ment, and to a man/woman the whole bunch of them failed to the extent that I only read their first two pitiful and facetious lines. They were thus obliged to do their write-ups from secondary sources, by word of mouth, which allowed for that mixture of spite, flip-pancy, distortion, baloney, occasional stab-in-the-dark random accuracy which being accurate by accident rather than intention is just as valueless as the usual lies and drivel.

However with regard to this matter of you being a profoundly uninteresting person. You still persist in thinking that I would like you in your short essay to impress me with your serious tastes in books, your addiction to fine classical music, the earnest news-papers and magazines you read and so on. To be frank, Mr Barkis, the fact you have waded through the entire Booker longlist as well as its shortlist this year strikes me as altogether far from original, being as it indicates you obviously seek refuge in fickle external authorities who come and go year by year to guide you in your tastes. All this means is that you cede your judgement to half a dozen folk who vary from overlauded and overpaid professors with vengeful bee-in-their-bonnet aesthetics, to cheerfully decerebrated pop stars whose notion of nuance is that it is a town in France or a type of depilatory cream. Why, as I urged you two years ago after your first application, do you not go to the public library and search ardently along its shelves sampling page by page what might be good and might be bad, using your own brain and your own coordinates to assess and discriminate? When you counter as you do by boasting that you have recently joined a Reading Group attached to said library, I'm afraid I all but throw up my arms in disgust. Need a bit of top tip guidance, some auxiliary cultural assistance as it were, Mr Barkis? Don't really know what to choose amongst the bewildering array on offer, so decide to get together with the retired doctor, the retired teacher, the house husband, the unemployed chap, the aroma-therapist lady, to chew away at the Booker shortlist 5/4 on favourite, with helpful notes at the back of the Penguin specially designed for the parched and famished Readers' Groups?

No point in rubbing it in further, but of the fifty writers you list as having read in the last twelve months I note that none of them are foreign, not a single one is pre-1950 much less nineteenth century or earlier. [If there was one dead foreigner, if for example you said with humble artless sincerity that you liked Turgenev's *A Sportsman's Sketches* because he seemed to actually like his more-than-flawed characters and that he had some affection for the world he knew in all its troubled glory] (*I hastily deleted this last unfinished sentence in case the bugger rushed out and bought* A Nest of Nobles *and got some brainy friend to lie about what Barkis thought about it*).

Combine that with the fact you are working your way through every single Mozart symphony on a CD package ordered from, it pains me to say those two appallingly conjoined words, Classic FM; have been to the last three queue-all-morning-to-have-any-hope-of-getting-in exhibitions at the Tate; are attending nightclasses to improve your French for the purpose of dedicated gourmet cheese-and-wine-study holidays; enjoy walking in the Lake District (and would love to go walking round the barely visited, hardly known, incomparable Debatable Lands of North East Cumbria if I would let you stay in The Lonning) . . . add all this together and I have this picture of compliant and affable and, forgive my candour, suffocatingly dull conformity.

Rather tetchily, it strikes me, you break down towards the end of your letter and demand to know what *really* are my criteria, that if your reading list and music lists and your admirable autodidact pursuits, and all that ramble, ramble rambling in the Lakes do not hold a candle, then what the hell *does* hold a candle for me, what do you, Mr Barkis, have to do, to stand a cat in hell's chance of eating and holidaying at The Lonning?

I suppose my answer, Mr Barkis, is that you can't do anything, there is a stony and immovable solipsism at work here. My honest guess is that you are an irremediably dull and conformist person, for all your many pursuits, for all your English degree, and your groundbreaking Open Univ. PhD thesis on how Mr Kingsley Amis compares with his contrasting son, and all the rest of it. But perhaps a more humane and kindly way of putting it in compelling analogical terms is this. A long time ago a friend of mine, a tradesman rather than an intellectual, a plumber in fact, though an unusual plumber inasmuch as he read a great deal and in his spare time produced highly original abstract paintings . . . this friend of mine gave me the odd news that apart from a cup of coffee for the last three years *he had entirely given up eating breakfast* . . . not a cornflake, not a single piece of toast, much less an egg or a rasher or a kipper had passed his lips for all that period!

I was most surprised on several scores, particularly as this burly sinewy friend was certainly the kind of person who looked as if he put away a Full English every morning of his life, and also because his job often demanded some heavy lifting and carrying which one would imagine would require a certain calorific baseline, a certain amount of energy-providing food inside his belly each morning. But in his very strong South London accent, he said, no he didn't feel weak with hunger after a hard morning's graft at his plumbing, and he insisted it had nothing to do with dieting or health reasons, his fasting. So why then, I persisted, had he *really* given up eating breakfast? Perhaps it was an over-reaction on my part but the answer when it came struck me as altogether remarkable. My friend said he had given up eating breakfast *because he knew precisely what it would taste like!* At this vatic, in my view truly mindboggling reply, I exclaimed with something of a transcendental illumination. What on earth did that mean, I pressed him with a certain desperation, as if afraid of not understanding something crucially significant? He sniffed and vehemently repeated that he couldn't be bothered with eating breakfast any more because he knew more or less exactly what to expect from the experience, and why should he bother with something where the experience was a foregone conclusion?

This then is my own borrowed aesthetic, my own number one selection criterion, Mr Barkis! I am afraid I am not willing, Mr Barkis (no pun intended!) to have you in my guest house, because in a nutshell I feel that I know *exactly* what your company will taste like, and as a result I can't be bothered to offer you my hospitality!

Sincerely
Joseph Gladstone
Proprietor

2

Contemporary broad Cumbrian dialect: *Missis Bessie Hodgin byakkt a maist tyasty plyat cyak.*

Hypothetical historical proto-Norse-Cumbrian: *Fru Bessie Hodgin bjakt a most tjasti pljat cjak.*

Standard English: *Mrs Bessie Hodgson baked a most tasty plate cake.*

The first mistake that any naïve soul might make is to believe that our Nordic strain, our Viking heritage, is mostly a matter of the archaic and rough-sounding vocabulary (*kyav, skop, lait, laik* etc.). Far from it. That is absolutely minimal child's play compared to the Nordic idiosyncrasies of the pronunciation.

Consider the identical 'a' sound in standard English *bake, tasty, plate* and *cake*. The Nordic, hence Cumbrian dialect corruption, of that 'a' sound is 'ya', pronounced as in *yap, yank, yahoo, yak, yarrow, Yamaha* etc. Alright so far, but now combine that same vowel with a preceding conso-nant, and you get *bya, tya, plya, cya* etc., the pronunciation and auditory comprehension of which defeats most deco-rous speakers of polite English who suddenly begin to feel they are in an Ingmar Bergman film where paradoxi-cally instead of grim tragedy the ambience is idiotic Cumbrian buffoonery. Instead of someone pondering whether to slit their throat or not against the backdrop of bare and pitiless Ibsenesque landscape, it is cheery Bessie H. gawping out the window at the backside of Skiddaw and baking her bloody old plate cake. Indeed the 'ya' sound on its own effortlessly explains the inevitably comic inflection of our oral and literary traditions. One only needs to meditate on the simple compound English binary word 'pasty-faced,' meaning 'wan', 'pallid of countenance' etc. In a standard English context the expression 'you look rather pasty-faced' is not remotely comic, but once Scandinavianised into broad Cumbrian dialect it becomes the contorted and infinitely expressive: *Thoo lyeuks raither pyassty-fyasst*. Which when uttered in a mock-solicitous you-look-not-far-from-a-one-way-ticket-to-hospital tone is bound to have us conspiratorially cackling at our quaint old argot.

Pyassty-fyasst. Can you say it? No, try again. Try saying, *pee-asty fee-asst*. Or *piasti fiasst*. No, try again. Try the hypothetical ur-Nordic version *pjasty-ffjast*. Come on, even a novice like you must have seen the hypnotic colour brochures for the Land of the Midnight Sun, and glanced at the sleeve notes on a Grieg record, and know how to say bloody 'fjord', don't you? Apparently not. You've maybe goggled at the glossy holiday brochures, but you've not learnt anything worth learning from the buggers. No, not bloody *fee-ord* . . . it's *fyord*. No, oh . . .

Let's move on.

Yesterday's dinner menu at The Lonning, 8 p.m., 6 December 2008

melitsanes sto fourno
(fried aubergine slices oven baked in a rich tomato sauce amply sprinkled with feta and nutmeg)

anginares yemistes
(globe artichokes boiled then stuffed with a mixture of walnuts, breadcrumbs and coriander leaf. Then covered with Greek white sauce [*aspri saltsa*] and grated cheese and baked for half an hour)

bamies me verikokka a la Kyrios Joe Gladstone
(okra with fresh apricots stewed in a basil and tomato sauce)

piperies yemistes
(green peppers stuffed with rice, tomatoes and chick peas flavoured with oregano. Baked in an aromatic tomato sauce containing basil, cinnamon and sugar)

kounopidhi tiganites
(cooked cauliflower florets fried in a rich egg, butter and milk batter)

kolokithakia yiahni
(zucchini braised in onions and tomatoes and sugar and flavoured ever so delicately with mint and dill)

This is just half the array of savoury dishes provided for last night's Greek banquet main course. For starters I made a mouthwatering medley of balls, if you'll pardon the expression (you and those bloody old balls of yours, as Liz never tires of reiterating). Which is to say *revitho keftedes, patates keftedes, spanakokeftedes, kolokithi keftedes* and *domatokeftedes*: chickpea balls, potato balls, spinach balls, zucchini balls and pain in the arse if wondrously succulent tomato balls, a literal ballsache if ever there was as you have to be a genius not to have your balls all aqueous and sludgelike no matter how dab your hand be with the tomatoes and the flour and the chopped onion.

For dessert, a choice of baklava, loukomades and halva. Followed by Greek coffee and Metaxas if so desired. Wine throughout good Kourtaki or Liokri retsina, like it or lump it, there may be a fine Greek red somewhere to be had in the UK but if there is I've no idea where, certainly not on the heaving booze shelves of Carlisle's Asda or Tesco. Apropos the controversial subject of retsina, Lawrence

Durrell, who was patently as addicted to it as Liz and I are, once wrote that those who loathe it variously compare it to turpentine and/or something strained through a bishop's socks. As he rightly adds, the glorious pine-resinated vinous nectar can only properly be experienced in Greece itself. True, these North East Cumbrian uplands might offer an infinitely tender and transcendent landscape, and we might have pine forests here in commercial abundance, but that's not the same as aromatic Greek pine forests, nor is the climate, consisting frequently of a stanchless North Cumbrian rain pissing from the perpetual grey and white skies, the same as the lustrous Hellenic variant.

Now then. I almost forgot to give you the menu, no I mean the *list*, of my house guests.

Bill Pargeter. Age, early forties. Accent, strongly Mancunian. Appearance, sturdy, tall, responsive, resilient. Occupation, self-employed all-purpose handyman in Oldham. Handbill promotional material. No job too small! No job too big! Will have a go at anything, and if I don't know how to do it, I will find out the best method from a book or through asking someone who knows more than I do. Cheap, reliable, friendly. Hobbies/interests. Remarkable. He has a Harley Davidson the size of a Buick on which in his extensive and expansive holiday periods he tours every part of the British Isles, visiting the homes, of would you believe it, illustrious dead musicians, artists, writers, scientists etc. Before and after these visits he listens to and reads up and watches illustrative videos and DVDs on variously Elgar, Delius, Dickens, Austen, George Eliot, D H Lawrence etc. At table he talks about all of them with great matter of fact and unschooled interest and enthusiasm, quoting the authorities who make sense to him but stating simply and sincerely his own feelings and opinions like that fabled vanished animal, a genuine autodidact. As far as bookish non-vocational courses go, surely the WEA is as dead as a doornail here and everywhere else in 2008, and yet Bill

Pargeter at my North Cumbrian table is effectively his own WEA. If he hadn't turned up on my doorstep after passing my entrance test, the short essay, I would not have credited his existence. He left school at sixteen so by rights he should find reading *Little Dorrit* an epic and impossible feat, instead of which he swallowed it voraciously rump and stump, if that's not a dubious metaphor from a vegetarian chef. Re-reading what I've just written about him, I simply don't believe it, meaning I don't believe Bill Pargeter: he must be factitious, an invention, a bit of rosy novelistic wishful thinking, not a man of flesh and blood. Because I half thought as much when I read his entrance exam, his essay, I decided I *must* rather than might have him here as a guest, so that I could give him a close and critical examination and decide whether or not he was a fraud. Assuming he just possibly wasn't, I needed to bag this rare Harley-propelled butterfly species before it disappeared.

Last night he looked at me across the table and I noted he had all four kinds of keftedes inside his mouth at once. He looked like some provocative experiment in artistic chromatography, with the palpating fusions of green courgette, the greener spinach, the red tomato and the fawn chickpea. He reminded me of my benefactor Uncle Harrison whom I once in the early Fifties saw manufacture a sandwich with ten different ingredients, one of which it pains me to say was cold black pudding and if that makes you heave be aware that the sandwich also contained greengage jam, condensed milk, dripping, Tate and Lyle's golden syrup . . . and polony.

After a masticatory gulp that would have broken my jaw had it been mine, Pargeter said: 'You know that I'm not a vegetarian.'

'No,' I said. 'I realise that. But you are while you're here.'

'Too damn right I am and gladly. But it's such a revelation to me, all this gourmet vegetarian grub of yours. I have friends who are serious veggies, plenty of them. But their food isn't anything at all like this, Joe. It's more like–'

Sixty-year-old Cora Dorr, who works in a supportive capacity in a refugee assessment centre stuck out in the middle of nowhere in marshy Lincolnshire, said: 'More like a species of punishment, the food they give you? I'd say the same. In fact until I stayed here . . .'

I snorted. 'It's one of the bees in my bonnet. Or maybe I mean one of the bees in the numerous hives owned by a notional apiarist magnate, all of which corresponds, to sustain the metaphor, to the bonnet of yours truly. Now then–' and I came to an abrupt and seemingly cul-de-sac halt.

Pargeter looked at me diagnostically, a middle-aged handyman autodidact surveying a pisswise elderly Oxbridge type. 'I do believe he's forgotten what he's going to say. You know, you're a very intelligent man, but the trouble with putting everything in brackets and then more brackets and then more brackets like you do, Joe . . .'

'Another issue altogether. Digressions are the staff – not stuff, staff – of life and anyone who tells you otherwise has never lived. No, the bee in my bonnet is that the worst advert for poor old vegetarianism is the bloody vegetarians themselves. Aside from their frequent unctuous sanctimoniousness, not to speak of their sickly complexions, there is the fact that barely one in a hundred can cook interesting cosmopolitan cuisine. Instead, as a rule they resort to lacklustre imitative meat cookery, a sort of Second World War austerity approach.'

'Mock goose,' said Marjorie Staff who is ninety-five and had just flown back from seeing her ninety-year-old kid sister in South India. 'The trouble is you know that lentils are not a goose, no matter how much the government then would have liked them to be so. They don't look like a goose and they don't taste like goose, not even slightly. The mock, you know, always seemed to suggest we were being mocked by the government civil servants rather than it being a coy reference to the ingredients.'

'Things haven't changed,' I growled. 'Go in any average wholefood shop and they have vegetarian sausages and vegetarian bacon, and *Quorn*, God save us, that would try to seduce you as mock chicken or mock mince. See what I mean. Playing second fiddle to Good King Meat, apologetic veggies pimping for unapologetic carnivores if you'll excuse my crude participle, parson.'

William Dixon, who at fifty-odd is a lay reader clergyman, replied: 'Not at all. You really needn't edit your language for me.'

'And stop calling him parson with the cheeky quote marks clanging around it every time,' said Liz. 'I know it's all meant as a joke but maybe he–'

I said, 'I once got thrown out of a London healthfood shop for asking why, given their sumptuous Quorn bacon and Quorn sausage array, they didn't bother to stock Quorn tripe, Quorn brains, Quorn cheek and Quorn testicles.'

'Ah,' said Marjorie and the dolmades she was eating suddenly seemed to fight back indignantly at her jaw rotations.

'Don't be so little boy disgusting,' snorted Liz. 'And it was a fit of Dutch courage if ever there was. He'd been drinking in a Chalk Farm wine bar all lunchtime and would have argued with a twenty-stone bouncer.'

'Nut roast works on the same laughable principle,' I persisted. 'It's mock mince casserole, and is not a patch on the original meat prototype. Ditto for aptly named "mush" stroganoff and vegetable (mock mince) lasagne, the twin veggie staples of deracinated and disgraceful public-house cuisine. I once got thrown out of a so-called select pub in Edgbaston for pointing out that same home truth.'

At which point Bill Pargeter asked me how many places I had been thrown out of in my seventy-three years and I answered no more than about five a year from the age of about twenty onwards.

The broad-minded parson said, 'Two hundred and fifty in total? And were you ever banned from any of them for good?'

'Only about fifty, and most of them outside the county, thank God. I prefer not to soil my home patch. No, the point I'm getting at is meat sausages are always going to taste better than plagiarist veggie sausages, because sausages are historically and rightly a meat dish, they are meat stuffed inside a skin literally. Hence the irony of some vegetarian fool paying three times as much for gourmet veggie Lincolnshires in a wholefood shop as he would for gourmet carnivorous Cumberland sausage in the butcher's next door. This decadent veggie eejit turns vegetarianism into a pampered and effete and very expensive bit of compromised nonsense. Instead, what this fool should be doing . . .'

I paused to swallow about a hundred and fifty ccs of Kourtaki then saluted the glass, it tasted so damn good.

'What?' asked Cora Dorr. 'What should he be doing? What should we all be doing?'

'We should take a leaf out of your own book, Cora. Don't look so mystified, I think you can guess what I am talking about. You spend your time working with trauma-tised foreigners who are being harshly vetted to see if they may be allowed to partake of our Anglo-Saxon bounty under such and such rigorous and precise and mean-spir-ited terms. What I'm saying is we should be generously cosmopolitan in outlook rather than pathetically derivative and imitative in our attitudes. This applies both to govern-ments apropos their tougher-than-thou ordinances about race and origin and refugee status, and cooks in the kitchen who are trying to be vegetarians. Don't imitate English meat cookery by cooking Quorn masquerading as chicken, but instead navigate ye boldly around the world and cook those foreign dishes where the demon meat be wholly absent!'

Pargeter was evidently wrestling with something. 'You

must mean that we need to go away and study lots and lots of cookbooks. You don't,' he wondered with a hopeful gleam in his eye, 'mean that we need to actually go out collecting recipes in Vietnam, Mongolia, Turkmenistan . . . ?' 'No,' I said. 'No we don't. Not even on a 2000 cc Harley Davidson. We just need to get ourselves some very good recipe books, and then start using the damn things. This is all a minefield of course, as some of the very best cookery writers, old and new, are inveterate meat enthusiasts. Fortunately as a rule, and Elizabeth David is a good example, the same folk tend to take an equal amount of trouble with their vegetables. The point is, if you want to eat well as a vegetarian, you have to cook on an *ethnic* basis, not on a bad imitation of meat basis. Once you have made that crucial decision, certain apparent problems are only theoretical. Any imbecile in possession of even the meagrest tastebuds would agree that Indian vegetarian cuisine is unparalleled. Poverty is an urgent educator of course, and it is astonishing what they can do with a few spices and a handful of peas or even the leafy tops of vegetables. In Bengal they can even make gourmet dishes out of marrows and anyone who can make anything out of a bloody old marrow is not a cook, he or she is a magician. Hence anyone who is partial to sub-continent cuisine is never going to miss dirty old meat or filthy old chicken. Ditto with vegetarian Chinese food which is surprisingly unexplored outside its native land. The real thing in all its daunting variety is nothing like those monotonous confections they serve in Chinese restaurants here: sweet and sour mixed veg, mixed veg chow mein, curried mixed veg etc. Instead of that we need to greedily sample, and to name at random, *La Zhi Bhicai, Jiang Bao Quiezi Pian, Longxucai Shao*, if we wish to know our arse from our elbow culinarily speaking.'

Marjorie Staff said swiftly, 'One hopes you don't stir your pans with either.'

I beamed at her as if infinitely charmed, and gave as ribald a retort as I could muster. Meanwhile Pargeter was surveying her obliquely, as if surprised that a very posh and elegant female in her nineties would ever indulge such an amiable coarseness.

'How do they translate?' Cora Dorr asked. 'I've got a pen. Can you—?'

'The first is Chinese cabbage fried with ginger, green chillis and carrot, then briefly stewed in sugar, vinegar and chilli oil and optionally garnished with sesame seeds. It is a truly delicious Sichuan recipe. The second is aubergine in brown bean sauce. The main thing is the eggplant is cut into thin strips, like long fat matchsticks, a technique unknown outside of China as far as I know, and it certainly makes a difference to the pungency and the tantalising flavour. The last one is asparagus Peking-style would you believe? The technique is similar to the cabbage dish but it is rice wine instead of vinegar that is mixed with the sugar. The asparagus needs to be parboiled, before the stir fry. You can always resort to rough sherry if your local Spar is out of rice wine. The rougher the better in fact. It makes a more than acceptable substitute in my view.'

'Bloody hell,' said Bill Pargeter.

'Quite,' I said.

'I don't actually like asparagus,' said Marjorie guiltily, as if she were severely letting the vegetarian team down.

'Neither do I,' I reassured her. 'It's the one and only vegetable I can't stand. But you can't always cook for yourself, can you? You have to think about others now and again.' I paused and played a soundless drum roll with my fork. 'Isn't that true, Liz?'

My wife shot me an angry glance as if she understood the far from veiled allusion. The rest of them at The Lonning's groaning board seemed to notice nothing and waded into their Greek tucker devotedly and in hungry silence.

* * *

41

Elizabeth, I mean Liz, might be seventy-three, but she has very recently betrayed me with another man.

Further instalment of *Galluses Galore*

The county was in a muted uproar (*aw Cummerlan wuss turnt upside doon on its heed, but cos ev its lang an pitifel histry ev adaptif passfizm nut ter menshun adaptif pess-mizm, wuss mekkin neah greet fash aboot it*). It was the overwhelming practical problems of implementing the Obligatory Braces Act that had everyone in a stew (*a weel nyamt an varra hortentick Cummerlan Styeub*). For a start, by January 2018 braces were not exactly a standard male fashion item, not even in a retrograde backwater like Cumbria. Old-fashioned gentlemens' outfitters in Working-ton, Whitehaven, Carlisle, Ambleside etc. initially did a gleeful, roaring trade then rapidly ran out of stock. While the one remaining braces supplier in the country, a four generations family concern down in Scunthorpe, worked overtime to meet the anomalous Cumbrian demand, still thriving galluses factories in Albania, Slovakia and other parts of Eastern Europe filled up capacious Transit vans three times a week and told their drivers to drive like the wind until at long last they got to the central Cumbrian braces supply depot in . . . the obscure little village of Frizington . . . (*t'factry manisher gadgers in Battyslaver, Tranny, Chestnut, Keef, Minshk, Pinshk, Buckrest, Warshy an sek like spots tellt their drifers ter up sticks an flee like buggery ter Frizzinton near Whitehebben in Inglish Cummerlan, else there'd be neah Nyoo Ear bowness and neah udder bliddy pucks, if they ed owt ter dyeuh wid it!*).
    These twenty-five-year-old Tirana, Kiev, Chishnau etc. braces executives being stridently competitive managerial tyros, restless Malthusians to a man, they were adamant that maximum haste with minimal tea breaks was the way

to outsmart all other East European suppliers (*an they sez, git thisel ter Cally, tyan t'bowt till eider Dowfer er Fyeukstyan, an still wit t'clog presst doon, drife like bliddy ell till thoo gits till t'A66 turrn off. Than, widoot drawn bread, clatter on ter Lyak Distickt Cockermoot, an think on an diven't thee dare stop theer! juss tyan strait on alang t'A5086 till lezhndry laal Frizzinton*). As for Frizington, having looked on its nifty little link to the Copeland council website (*a varra pleasin ter naffyget webshite*) the Tirana, Kiev etc. tyros were amazed to see that the Second World had its economic, cultural and indeed architectural representatives in the West as well as in the East (*an they sez till t'wurrit-lyeukin curriers, Thoo'll syeun feel at yam theer, cos this comickal laal spot lyeuks juss like tippercal Albany, Bellyrushing, Polony, Tuckmanystyans, but mebbe a laal bit wuss off if ah's been breutal oppchecktif as a leadin Seckent Wurld galluses factry manifacter*).

Logistics? Logistics, yes! Logistics Eastern European-style was the name of the game. But as for the daunting problems of actually enforcing the pilot-scheme Obligatory Braces Act in practice? The premier Thomas Purley (*t'top gadger Tommy Pullet*) had insisted that these experimental-scheme braces be seen to be visible at a glance on all Cumbrian males. Which was emphatically easier said than done, if you were one of the special constables who had been put on split-shift braces vigilante duty as every one of the Cumbrian specials had been for the last few weeks. It might be easy enough in summer when many of these typical Toms, Dicks, Harrys (*paradickmatic Cummerlan marraboys Arrison, Jakie, Pyurt an Tucker*) would be strolling in their shirtsleeves to identify their tell-tale suspenders, but this was at the start of January and it was freezing cold. Plenty of these Cumbrian chaps wore thick sweaters as well as shirts underneath their jackets or coats, so how were the mandatory braces to be made visible underneath all that quantity of camouflage?

In the end the Whitehall civil servants came up with two ingeniously creative options apropos the business of inclement weather and braces:

1. If on account of the weather or any other natural and unforeseen constraint the pilot-scheme individual be wearing a braces-concealing overcoat, windcheater or waterproof, the overcoat must be tucked completely inside the top of the trousers and the braces placed externally and suspended on the shoulders of the overcoat. This shall henceforth be called the Shoulder Suspension Option (SSO).

2. If on the other hand the coat be so bulky and the trousers so snug-fitting that it is physically impossible to stuff the former inside the latter, then the loops of the braces must be pulled though a hole or gap half way down the coat, windcheater or waterproof. Then, because these loops obviously cannot be suspended over the now constricted shoulders, they must be separated and parted just below the wearer's neck. For want of any other convenient suspension device they must then be looped securely and conspicuously over the pilot-scheme individual's ears (*they ev ter hing fizzable till t'nyakkt eye ower t'strainin marra-boy's lyeugs*) which must be caused to protrude should this be essential to facilitate a firm grip (*ter git a gud tight hod on t'galluses lasstick*). This alternative shall henceforth be designated the Ear Suspension Option (ESO).

You get the urgency of the drift, do you? Once again it is logistics we are talking about (*yon bliddy owd loadshit-sticks we carn't tyan oorsels awae frae up in progress-mad Cummerlan!*). Two weeks after Christmas then, here we are in, to take any small Cumbrian town at random, Aspatria (*Spyatri*), notable for its erstwhile prominence in the national newspaper weather reports, its buoyant (!) mattress factory (*sister an attractif laal lake on woods*) and the pasteurised creamery that is pleasingly conspicuous from its railway station. Half of these Aspatrian adult

44

males, it will be observed (*lookster t'bliddy cut on yon*), are walking around in unseasonable shirtsleeves. Their braces are certainly visible at a glance, but these doughty galluses-wearers are shivering violently in the freezing cold. They do this, one might hazard, out of a vestigial modicum (*a mottycombe ev a mottycombe*) of sartorial self-respect, because the other half of the Aspatria males are, to put it mildly, a fascinating anthropological phenomenon. A sulking majority of these are SSOs walking around with overcoats stuffed clumsily and resentfully inside their pants, and looking like so many parodies of Michelin men who happen to have farcical galluses wrapped tight about their indignant clavicles. But a mindboggling minority are dressed as that traffic-halting spectacle, an ESO, meaning he who looks like a quaint caricature of a Beano character (*t'Bash Stert Bairns like Smiffy er Wilferd er laal Oorpert wit t'greet glassis, skwint ice, centre partin, an t'smart Heaton syeut*). In the ESO's case, a nice little Burton's or Burberry top coat is weirdly bifurcated in the neck region by a kind of comic garrotte (*byfyeukt bi a funny laal carrot*) which is then tautened after the manner of odd-looking spectacle arms across the Aspatria man's blushing ears (*t'Spyatri gadger's pertyeudin an raither bashfel lyeugs*).

It is true to say that these pilot-scheme subjects, some of whom were as blue as icicles, some of whom felt and looked like Mr Blobby and others like Bash Street's Herbert or Smiffy, were not really enjoying being guinea pigs. Even though they had been told they were doing their nation an inestimable service in 2018, they were not unqualifiedly happy in their pioneering sociological roles. The Whitehall chaps had made detailed provision to monitor the incidence of male Cumbrian vandalism, streetfighting, football hooliganism, committing a public nuisance (*pishin up agyan t'wo when thoo's tight, er mebbe nut seah tight, juss bliddy aunty soshal*) over the next twelve months. One incidental irony was that in 2018 a great many of these pilot-scheme chaps' wives were having the times of their lives in another homophonous context. In the local FE centres they were attending 'Pilates' classes where they would learn inner calm, spiritual serenity and how to acquire smaller backsides (*thoo'll feel aw roont yoophorick, mi lass, cos at lang last thoo hess a behint thoo's nut embarrasst aboot*). Not for them humiliating government-ordained compulsory fashion, but a voyage of transcendental self discovery and smaller buttocks, and to be honest many of them barely noticed that their husbands were going about like so many trussed and staggering circus clowns.

Most of these pilot-scheme males went about muttering resentfully as who would not in their anomalous circumstances? But none of them wanted to be fined for discarding their Scunthorpe, Tirana, Chishnau etc. braces and still less of them wanted to languish in Haverigg or Durham jails, or it was rumoured, not without anticipatory terror, be microchipped and forced to stay at home between 6 p.m. and 6 a.m. for a month (*neah neet time pub, neah neetcap yal, neah pullerlatin fiebrant dockermentry style solt ev t'uth nordern fwoak gollerin Perry Manylove in t'Wukkin Mens*). So they all to a man had muttered and put up with it, all over Christmas and New Year, just as Cumbrians have been muttering and putting up with things and trudging on since time immemorial (*they carry on raither like they div in fyatalistick Delly and Calcutter cept they carnt blyam their religion er poorsnal filosofy fer that*). Some might say this sociological trait of extreme passivity is a function of not one but two critical economic recessions: the one the whole country knew about circa the mid-1970s, and the far worse one Cumberland suffered at the start of the twentieth century. Some might add that the passivity is accompanied by a certain functional and structural and even genetic complacence (*we're nut owny med the way we're med, but it syeuts us in marraboy aunty pology Lefty Stroos's fyamous teary, ter be the way we bliddy well are*). Whatever the case, it is instructive that even in a closed structural system where people only function in terms of reciprocal relationships (*eggsistunsbal haughtynomie bein owny a pitifel bliddy mirage*) one individual at least will rise up in rebellion.

Oh? At least one? Is that a fact (*is yon as true as thoo's sittin theer?*). And was there one on the aqueous Cumbrian skyline in 2018? If so, what was this quirky and headstrong (*kwucky an heedstrang*) rebel's name?

His name was Fenton Baggrow (*Fenton wuss his mudder's myaden nyam, and Baggra near Spaytri wuss where his gurtgurtgurtgurtgurtgurt an mebbe ten mare gurts grandfadder wuss a pheasant-vessel-surf in gey primtiff Cummerlan in aboot 1066 A.D.*).

Oh really? And what was his occupation, this singular rebel called Baggrow?

None (*Nin. Bugger aw. Ee did nowt. Ee ligged aboot bwoan idle, as bowld as bliddy brass*). For most of the day and every day, Baggrow sat idling in the pub where he was seen to consume about twenty-five pints of beer without haste and most puzzlingly without shortage of cash. No one had any idea where his income came from, and the surmise was that it was some sort of inheritance, even though his poor-as-a-churchmouse parents had both been on long-term sickness benefit because of a complementary alcohol addiction. It should be noted that this long-dead couple's offspring Fenton did not patronise the one pub, but on a daily basis and using a sturdy bicycle moved about the extended North East Cumbrian terrain, all around the Brampton and Longtown areas, and also along the A689 Brampton to Alston highway axis (*them run doon but gran owd ostelries in sek as Tintle Fell, Mitch Howm, Gilda Dyal, an Lidget*).

And what was Fenton Baggrow's specific method of rebellion?

He sat in his shirtsleeves, flagrantly and insolently minus

any braces (*ee wore neah galluses. As bowld as bliddy brass*). While everyone else was stiff with apprehension when the special constables came in on vigilante duty, he would cackle and hurriedly slip into the public-house conveniences. There using a joke-shop product from a bulk supply kept in his rucksack, he would pour a hideous liquid down the lavatory bowl which would keep the specials and everyone else for that matter out of the pub bog for the next two hours at least. The joke-shop liquid was some sort of organic mercaptan derivative (*ethel or methel or mebbe sek as highsobootin wassacomie moorcaptain, an it stunk like ten thoosand orrible farts frae a sherryhatrick cuddy wid colic*).

Crikey. And did he infect any of the other local men with his seditious behaviour?

He did his damn best! He certainly lectured his co-drinkers, all obediently be-gallused, on what he termed their adaptive historical quietude (*we've menshunt Oorpert frae t'Beano but wat aboot t'uther Oorpert, yon Markoozy interlekshal perfusser gadger frae Buckley, Callyfongy?*) their cowardice, their lack of political grasp, their blindness to where all this obligatory, compulsory this and that, was leading not just them, but the whole of the country, most of Europe, and a fair cross section of the globe come to that! First of all it had been five compulsory pieces of fresh fruit (*five pisses ev happel, orinsh, gyeusgog, sherry an aw wat nut*) and now it was strap on your obligatory braces or jail! How much more could he or they possibly take?

So what exactly did this all amount to, I can hear you ask, apropos frontline confrontational politics in pilot-scheme Cumbria in January 2018?

I'm afraid you will have to wait and see (*sister, thoo'll hev ter bide thi time an hod thi bliddy watter*).

End of instalment of *Galluses Galore*

3

Once my son Desmond when he was about thirteen years old came to me with a dog-eared paperback copy of *Peyton Place* by Grace Metalious, and asked me an innocent question. He wanted to know what on earth that bizarre ten-times-a-page word 'sonofabitch' meant. Much to my amusement, he pronounced it 'sono-fay-bitch' as if it had something to do with sleek and idealistic English Fabians romping and disporting themselves all over Ms Metalious's remarkable pages. Of course he realised it was a term of abuse when applied to all and sundry as it was in steamy New England, especially to that horny Greek doctor whose name escapes me some half a century after its publication. Nonetheless he thought it a very grotesque and laborious single-word insult.

I had to point out that it was four words flushed into one by some coyly prudish Sixties copy editor, and as illiterate and absurd as some *Boy's Own* swashbuckling hero bawling the preposterous 'sonofadog' (mediaeval Welsh?) at his ignoble opponent on the poop deck. The adult logic, I told him, was that if the words were flushed together they became some sort of semantic fudge and ceased to be as offensive as the separate words. Clearly it had worked in Desmond's case as he really thought there was such a weirdly agglutinated Yankee insult. It put me in mind, I told him nostalgically and with genuine fatherly feeling, of that time five years earlier when I had noticed him carefully reading a notice on the inside of the double-decker bus we had taken into Carlisle. Once we had got off it, he had asked me why the number of people you could safely get on the bus was called its 'capper-city'. He simply couldn't understand the semantic connection with – looking wonderingly at bleary Sixties Carlisle – what he understood by the word 'city'.

'You remember,' I teased him playfully in this would have been about 1973 or 1974. 'I had to get you to practise saying "ca-PA-city", not "ca-pa-CITY", about half a dozen times, and even then you didn't understand why milk in bottles and people in a double decker could be described by the same word.'

Desmond the sullen sex-starved adolescent glowered at me then and pointed out that it was no sin to be naïve at eight years old, nor at thirteen was he required to be some language expert who was supposed to be able to decode words which had been artificially flushed together. At this point I became mildly combative when really I was feeling stung, even hurt, by his response. I ought to have left it at that I suppose, but I always feel obliged to pursue my case to the end, even with those who are a third of my age. I couldn't resist reminding him of that memorable time when aged six in 1966 he had tried to impress his infants' teacher with a story full of a wondrously precocious vocabulary. We had recently been reading *Just William* books together at his bedtime, and inspired by that, in his little tale about a chivalrous knight called Cyril, he had described his upright but touchingly all too human hero as being 'suspectible' to feminine charm. What had made me chuckle all the more was that Miss Amelia Burrows had subsequently given him a big tick and a golden star, commending him rapturously for the big word which she for one hadn't realised was a mistake.

Desmond probably doesn't resent me all that much, or at least Liz assures me he loves me like any son loves his father, despite those studied and subtly guarded exchanges he offers whenever we meet face to face. The roles have been reversed to a certain extent as he is the pragmatic, salaried and successful professional down there in Wiltshire, while old pop is the improvident fathead who runs a loss-making guest house in the remote sticks and spends his spare time writing cookbooks nobody buys, composing nonsense in a dialect not many understand, and jotting down far from gripping pensées about things not even as riveting as train numbers, viz. binary words.

Which is why in the first place I started this meditation on 'son of a bitch'/'sonofabitch' which is an ext. like a 1 of 2. Before I start on about a real ext. like a 1 of 2 called Patrick Garnett who has recently captured the imagination of a woman called Liz Gladstone, I should point out that dog binaries are perhaps the most fascinatingly ambiguous and nuanced of all. This seems to be at least in part because of the degree to which dogs are either idolised or despised by the fickle human race. Right enough the non-binary term of abuse 'dog' has been around since the dawn of time, and binary correlates would include 'sly dog' when used in its pejorative sense, though it can of course be used approvingly of some non-canine 'waggish' rake. Sly dog is ext. as 1 as a 2; and we also have 'son of a dog' which is a rather less vehement insult than 'son of a bitch', 'dirty dog', 'vile cur', 'fawning cur' etc. When by contrast human-kind decides to identify itself sympathetically with its staunch old companion the dog, we get 'dog days' which is an ext. like 2 of 1, the expressive 'dog tired' which is ext. as 2 as 1, the problematic 'hangdog' and that most endearing of all binaries, canine or not, 'gay dog' . . .

That last one needs no introduction, nor for that matter should it ever see a semantic conclusion. Have you ever watched a dog that is dementedly happy, tearing aeronau-tically, lugs at full-splayed tension, about the field or the lawn in a way that would touch the stoniest, meanest heart? Ever been as joyous as an innocent dog yourself, have you, stout citizen of 2008? Desmond Gladstone was when he was four or five years old, with a wild, liberated, couldn't-give-a-damn guffaw if ever there was. I am moved more strongly than I care to be by the pricking memory and wonder like any open-mouthed naif how it is that a cackling small boy, a perfect and pristine and promising young anarchist, should have metamorphosed into his present ossification as a Wiltshire market town Civic Centre Arts Manager who has won more commendations for packing them in to the CC than I have had lunches of hot courgette couscous (another CC).

As for 'hangdog' it is altogether the odd one out. I had hoped being a soft-hearted vegetarian that it was an ext. 1-ing like a 2, i.e. some sort of elliptical reference to the way a dog often droops in a touchingly melancholy and vulnerable manner when exhausted or waiting for a drink. Instead my dog-eared (ext. like a 2 of 1) dictionary, refers me to 1677 and gives the definition as a despicable chap 'fit only to hang a dog, or to be hanged like a dog'. Both images are infinitely abhorrent but the first one has me compendiously confused. Fit only to hang a dog . . . was that some sort of revoltingly unsentimental job in the old days delegated only to the lowest of the low, was there actually some kind of nightmarish canine gallows depot in lieu of the drowned-in-a-sack option?

But, as to my wife Liz. Let us first of all face a few prejudices and then both acknowledge and dispel them. How come, I ask myself, she decided to have her first affair in 2005 when she was seventy years old and after forty-five years marriage, after celebrating her polypropylene wedding or whatever the damn anniversary was (the pearl, the topaz, the luxury iPod, the mobile phone that makes real coffee)? This query of mine, such as it is, is ageist so they tell me, by which they mean the business of discriminating against a person on the grounds of advanced years. Let me stress then that I am not querying Liz's physical or mental capacity (q.v. Desmond's double-decker query of 1968) for embarking on an affair, but her moral position in this far from pretty matter. In any case, apropos ageism, it was only about three years ago that I was able to demonstrate my own impeccable credentials when it came to taking a public stand. In 2005, round about the time Liz must have been falling in love with Patrick Garnett, I was in a Carlisle electrical shop with forty-five-year-old Desmond when the youthful assistant tried to use the latter as Help The Aged go-between and cognitive auxiliary. He actually asked Des if 'he', meaning the wordless fly-catching dotard to his left, mightn't be safer with such and such a trip safety device in his kitchen. I turned furiously on the impudent little whelp, all sticky-up hair and glasses and looking at least ten, though he was probably about twenty-three or older.

'You won't be safe, sonny,' I growled, 'if you dare to treat me as a deaf and dribbling mute who needs his son to do the important stuff for him! Little boy, I am seventy not ninety-five, and in case you don't know it the average life expectancy in riproaring New Socialist UK is seventy-seven or seventy-eight these days. I doubt if you have much maths, but that statistical mean indicates that there must be a hell of a lot in their eighties and nineties who with a bit of luck will soon do you out of a job you don't deserve. Admittedly I know damn all about electrics or electrical safety, but then neither does this middle-aged stripling, my son. I have an electrician pal up country in the Bewcastle area who as it happens is seventy also, and so mentally alert I can assure you he gives off static electricity. While we're at it he has not one but *three* girl-friends, all of whom know about each other and none of whom are happy about it. Possibly it is something to do with the static electricity he gives off, a kind of force-field pheromone with knobs on. And be assured, young sales-man, that he doesn't sit doing brainless Puzzle Books with his North East Cumbrian fancy women on lethargic Sunday afternoons up in peaceful Bewcastle. He is still in full turgid vigour, sonny boy, and lets fly at these women like–'

I was yanked out of the electrical store by my middle-aged carer before I could be banned from it for life. Desmond would not speak to me for the next hour and was deeply embarrassed about my public claim, however obscure, and even though the public was only bloody old Carlisle, to a geriatric libido, to being a senile sexual being, to being the same as everyone else! There I was boasting admiringly about my friend Kenny the promiscuous electrician in his seventies, when the truth was my own timid monogamous behaviour was being outflanked by my sneaky little helpmeet Liz. That night she would attend a rock concert twenty miles away in a village hall stuck out in the wilds with two old girlfriends Jane and Marge. Also present was Jane's brother, a sixty-two-year-old babe-in-arms called Patrick Garnett. Nothing would happen that night as it happened, or rather nothing definite with regard to Garnett. Then a month after that she would go to another concert, music-mad Patrick would be there yet again with his sister, and this time Liz and he would dance together. To anticipate the pattern and your own impatience, these concerts which varied between rock, jazz, world music, salsa, rap and every damn thing barring Bartok, Max Bygraves and any other crooning balladeers, were regular monthly events, the first Saturday in all cases. I was usually busy with The Lonning and wouldn't have wanted to have gone to anything other than the jazz in any case. And so it went. And so it grew. I knew nothing at all about it until the end of 2007. It went on for one year, then two years, then . . .

* * *

'It began quite strangely. In one sense it was as if I and for that matter Patrick had nothing to do with the way things developed . . .'

I smiled sardonically. 'What the hell is that supposed to mean? Sounds like good old-fashioned wishy-washy sophistry to me.'

'I'm trying to be honest and you're trying to be hurtful. I mean that it took on its own overwhelming momentum. I did not want to fall for him, I really didn't. I don't really think he wanted to fall for me. I certainly fought against it and . . .'

What we are looking at is secondary reportage via Liz, the blow-by-blow confession of an unfaithful wife. It is second-hand vividness so to speak and I am obliged to see the scenario through her eyes as well as faithfully recount it, inasmuch as I understand it. Also most importantly I have to give an account of the first visit to this rustic rock venue when Patrick might have been there but Liz felt no immediate stirrings in his direction. The reason for this preliminary scene setting is that Patrick came in the wake of a vision, or one that I would circumspectly term a vision, though Liz remains uncertain about what exactly it might have been. The aftermath of that first rock concert was a kind of gentle shaking or crisis within my seventy-year-old wife's self or soul or whichever word is most accurate. It says much for my crassness that I didn't even notice the change in her, so preoccupied I was at the time with The Lonning, writing yet another cookbook that would likely vanish without trace, musing about binary compounds, drinking in lively Debatable Lands pubs with Casanova Kenny the electrician when I had nothing better to do etc.

First of all, let's get it straight in terms of the credible and the incredible. For all her sensitivity and considerable intelligence, Liz is a tough old nut and has no history of seeing things. She has spent plenty of nights on her own in a very old North Cumbrian farmhouse, and has never yet heard or seen anything that wasn't either a bird or a mouse or a midge or a stumbling drunk lurching home guffawing from a far-flung rural pub. Not even in her teens, when adolescent girls are supposed to take strange turns, did Liz ever think anything but two and two make four and there's an end of it. Like me she likes her wine but she is not a pig, not as big a guzzling bebbing pig as I can be at any rate. She didn't have post-natal depression with her only child Desmond, and the only thing that has ever really depressed her is that I have wasted so much of Harrison's legacy on that decadent exercise The Lonning. In part that is why I am busting a gut to win the fifty-grand prize with my dialect fable *Galluses Galore*. If and when I win it I will give it all to Liz, and say there, that is by way of compensation for heedlessly pissing away my inheritance. You ought to have been able to retire, Liz, I will remorsefully confess, with all that fortune from Uncle Harrison, though let's face it the idea of you doing nothing in your seventies is a joke. Every time you go in any room in any house in any part of the country, it is automatically redesigned, you even pull out a notepad and pencil and start realising the new improved version on the spot. Like the fabled bird-watcher/twitcher who will never be able to stop watching and twitching at each and every bird, you are an interior designer who will never be able to cease redesigning each and every interior.

The circumstances of my wife's vision were on the face of it banal. It was all to do with the rock band she was watching in the village hall. Here I need to be more specific with my terms and say that they weren't a rock band, they were a kind of boogie-woogie ensemble, meaning a thumping vibrant piano, a host of blaring raucous saxes, and the half dozen jigging male musicians were all attired in an extraordinary uniform. Unlike the original transatlantic exponents of boogie-woogie, these gentlemen were all Mancunians in their mid thirties, all white, all very talented according to Liz, but insufficiently commercial to have any hope of performing in the major venues. As a result their gigs were mostly in Manchester pubs and small towns in the north west of England, and last but not least go-ahead rural village halls in Lancashire, Yorkshire, Northumbria and Cumbria, i.e. wherever an adequate number of middle-class inroading professionals had settled in the rustic locale and could provide a staple and appreciative audience. Liz by the way learnt all of this rock-band sociology via Marge who during the interval had gone and chatted to the best looking of the band, the burly, bellowing and oddly serious-looking singer.

Speaking of looks, Patrick Garnett apparently wore three-hundred-pound designer denim jeans and a three-hundred-quid designer denim jacket and would have passed for fifty, Liz told me with a dispassionate inflection as if she was talking about prime pedigree stock or a new type of wood gloss.

'He was very good-looking, but then so were you at his age. Sorry, I didn't mean to say that. I mean you still are–'

'No I'm not. I am an ugly old goat of seventy-three who would pass for eighty-three in a bad light. Or even under full blaze halogen come to that, if I've been out on the tiles and hitting the pop.'

Pop was being hit by all but Liz that night. There was a frantically crowded bar where Patrick and sister Jane were buying brown ale and gin and tonic respectively. Jane runs a café just over the border in Northumbria and although she is sixty-eight has dyed red hair of a fetching and provocative lustre. Marge, who fronts an antique shop on the Scots side, asked for a glass of dry white which she immediately declared might once have been paint stripper. It didn't stop her drinking lots of paint stripper all night according to Liz, who as driver spent the evening on bottled water. The lighting in the old-fashioned hall which possessed a tea urn and umpteen ancient stacked wooden chairs, was red and dim, like a timeless teenage dance venue circa 1963. The red light fell on Patrick's designer accoutrements and full head of silver hair and Liz saw at once that he was attractive, though she firmly insisted that she was not drawn to him that night. That at any rate was what she repetitively told me in that hideous week of confession, though who is ever to know? Maybe she thought she wasn't when she was, perhaps her being seventy and him being early sixties but passing for fifty, the amorous coordinates were less clear and demarcated than she in retrospect assumes.

But enough of nuance, which can be both a salvation and a curse, and especially in matters of the heart. Let's talk about the band instead. The band were all dressed in the same uniform, and were attired as *clergymen*.

Sorry, accurate definitions again. They were all dressed to appear as Southern Baptist clergymen or just possibly the New Orleans variety, a cheerful conflation which wasn't going to matter that much. In reality they were all broad Mancunians pretending to be cornpone Flannery O'Connor or Truman Capote white preachers. They all wore dog collars, black tops and black trousers, and the name of their band was Reverend Wiley and the All Stars.

Ain't got no time to struggle and fight
I got my pride and I've seen the light

Which was one repetitive lyric that Liz recalled and sang for me with some effort. She wasn't sure if it was a standard or not, and as a boogie singer she frankly wasn't up to much. However these fervent Dixie preachers certainly gave it all they'd got. So far so good you might say. Remember Tarts and Vicars at old-fashioned fancy-dress parties? I never actually attended such a jovial shenanigan and was always strongly unimpressed by the notional satire. The weedy, prognathous, knock-kneed, lisping Anglican clergyman, mingler at lacklustre jumble sales, enthusiast at duck races and paper chases, judge of marmalade and chutney comps etc. is such an obvious clown of a target that the comedy is not there. Whereas, if from say 1960 onwards and for the next five seamy decades, the public had favoured fancy-dress ensembles of Tarts and *Politicians*, I might have been a little more impressed . . .

Turned upside down and filled with shame
I've got no home and got no name

And who might that refer to in the present scenario? After her confessional we were both turned upside down and in a state of shock, and the vertigo induced by a wounded heart is perhaps more pernicious at seventy than forty. But that is to anticipate, and I still have to set the scene of that first evening she had in Patrick's presence. The form of each musical number went as follows. The song would proceed as a vigorous and infectious boogie standard lasting perhaps ten to fifteen minutes. At a certain point there would be a lengthy sax solo followed swiftly by an improvised comic monologue from the singer, the eponymous band-leader, the Reverend Wiley. His monologues, according to Liz, were more or less unvarying in sentiment if slightly different in exposition each time. The gist of them was that the Reverend was tormented with unholy lust towards the more nubile members of his imaginary but vividly portrayed female flock, and for that matter every single attractive woman who came within his orbit. He would gurgle on with demented concupiscence about their curvaceous limbs and delectable appurtenances, and would mimic a fervent, lubricious drooling where the saliva was as torrential as a Mississippi waterfall. Here via Liz is a typical extract from his penultimate number that was sung at about half past eleven on that warm and vivid Saturday night, and when virtually everyone was dancing, Liz with addled Marge and Jane with her designer-clad brother Patrick.

'Sistah, lissen to me, you must lower yourself, you must *lower* yourself an surrendah your will! You must cast off your . . . you got to cast it off, sistah . . . and once you've cast it off, you have to *surrendah* everythin an . . .'

This from a Mancunian whose real name was probably Kevin and who was likely to be an art teacher with a mortgage from Didsbury. Was he on one level and unawares whispering his lewd thoughts into Liz's receptive subconscious as well as Patrick Garnett's designer subconscious (no doubt they'll have such things one of these days)? The final number when it came had everyone on the floor, the band was so intoxicated by its ferocious playing and singing, the audience so exalted by the passion of the music and the red-lit demi-monde ambience, not to speak of the Reverend who had reached such a phenomenal climax of jigging blurting eloquence. Nor could he resist talking about climaxes as a consequence. He orated at length about the matter, and then when the song was almost at an end mysteriously disappeared behind the band so that all the rapturous audience were heckling him to return.

'Where on earth's he gone?' said Patrick impatiently. According to Liz, this youthful sexagenarian was exceptionally lithe and tireless as a boogie dancer and showed every intention of twitching and twirling his way towards dawn.

'And what on earth is that in his hand?' hiccupped Jane who'd had a lot of gin and who suddenly started laughing uncontrollably.

The Reverend returned alright. He returned bearing a carrier bag, of all things. He started to fish inside it and the audience erupted as they assumed he had balloons for them to inflate or Smarties or penny whistles or streamers or something equally of the carnival.

'It's his bag of CDs,' opined Marge, rather sour by now after all that corrosive paint stripper. 'But I'm not going to buy one because they're never as good as the live performance. They're always a grave disappointment I've learnt by experience.'

But no, they weren't the Reverend's CDs, nor were they anybody else's. Out of the bag he brought not one, but three or four old . . . books.

His mostly literate audience sat up at that of course, even though almost every one of them – average age late thirties, early forties – was standing panting from all that dancing.

'Oh,' said Liz with a sudden acclamation in her voice she could barely understand.

He had done the skilled trick that all old pros, all performers, whether teachers or clowns or professors or TV jokers, do. He had produced the intriguing and enigmatic artefact, thereby at a stroke gaining the attention of his otherwise addled and puddled late-night audience. His books weren't just any old books either. It was fitting that Reverend Wiley's reading matter was what it was. The Reverend brought out a clutch of ancient Bibles. Which all looked to be of the economy variety, the kind you would acquire in a charity shop for a song. They seemed a bit dog-eared (ext. like a 2 of 1), as if part of a job lot from a Methodist chapel that had been converted into a house or a warehouse or a shop or anything but a House of God. They could have stood near the door in an RSPCA or Help The Aged charity shop in somewhere like say Whalley Range or Longsight or Didsbury, waiting hopefully for someone to come and buy them for fifty pence the lot.

The purchaser in this case happened to be Kevin, I mean Reverend Wiley, minus his All Stars.

Liz who was the only sober one of the four, assumed that he was going to read some Biblical verses on the spot, and for no reason she could make clear to herself was looking forward to it. She took it for granted that even he, even the stocky boogie jester here, would not think to mock or traduce or distort what he was holding in his hands, not even here, not even now, not even among this obviously secular but clearly decent-hearted audience of a hundred or so middle-class liberal professionals.

He did more than that. Reverend Wiley walked round the free space in the village hall *tearing up* the charity-shop Bibles . . .

By now he had stopped all singing, ceased all hectic monologuing, it was the end of the night, time for the instrumental finale. To the accompaniment of the blaring saxes, he tore up the carrier-bag Bibles one after another into dozens of shreds, and flung all the paper behind his head. Liz assured me that it did not come across as vengeful or deliberate so much, as without any authentic connection between the deed and the man. It was – what was the word? – a *gesture*. An act that is which the Reverend knew to be provocative in theory, but which, being without any instinctive sense of the reverential himself, as he did it seemed as gestural and inconsequential as any other formulaic action.

Before long there was a confetti of scripture all over the dance floor. Liz, who has never ever been a believer and who in her seventy years has only been to church about a dozen times for weddings and funerals and christenings, was shocked to the core. Interrogate her why she should have felt so traumatised and she is hard put to be precise about the wherefores. But it was so wholly unexpected. It was so completely out of the blue. Even more shocking, she said, was that no one else on the dance floor seemed remotely perturbed. As if all it was was an empty gesture relating to something about which they knew almost nothing, even though, they dimly recalled, an irrational tiny minority took it all very seriously. After all there could have been two or three alternative gimmick endings to the performance, but instead there was this one . . . act of violence . . . which Liz felt herself objecting to instinctively. Surely the Reverend Wiley could have opted to follow the logical conclusion of his suggestive monologues, taken all his clothes off, and performed a rumba-cum-boogie that would have more than satisfied his audience, and especially Marge who was openly delirious about his physique. And if that wasn't going far enough, then he could have aped or even performed jovial copulation on the dance floor with a willing participant and who is to say Marge full to the gills with paint stripper might not have obliged?

Instead of which he had switched parodic roles and become not a book burner but a book destroyer. And as I say it was not just any old book, not *Silas Marner* or *Das Kapital* or *Gone to Earth* or *Gone with the Wind* but the . . .

Liz became deeply upset. She believed she was the only one here tonight to feel anything like this, and as a result felt isolated and wholly estranged. She was like a forlorn child who had been frightened or even terrified at a party or in a playground. She left dancing with Marge and walked around the floor pretending to be very happy to twirl on her own, but actually very busy scrutinising the devastation at her feet. In the dim and hallucinatory pink light she saw shreds of single verses, shreds of part verses, pairs of verses. She was very specific about what it was she saw. What she saw on her patch of the floor were shreds of the Epistles, the Letters of Saint Paul. She saw little bits of Ephesians. She noticed little pieces of Colossians. She saw them thrown down there regardless on the dusty old village hall floorboards. Miraculously, most of the verses though shredded were still entire.

And then she had her vision.

Looking down through the hallucinatory but tender pink light, my wife saw these bits of verses glowing with a delicate white light, with an endless and infinitely gentle radiance. For an age the world to all its limits stood still and simply breathed. Within the space of a second she, my wife, understood, and not in words, at least five important things:

–that this gentleness visible now as delicate radiance was infinite.

–that it was eternally indestructible.

–that it offered neither retaliation nor vengeance to the individual who had tried to damage it.

–that above all and related to all of the above, this gentleness was infinitely beautiful.

–that the notions and nouns of gentleness, infinity and beauty were not of our ordinary human quantification, understanding or qualitative evaluation. Instead, they were from somewhere else.

'I was watching a kind of stream or current of quite incredible gentleness radiating from those little bits of paper on the floor. Even though the stream was invisible and immaterial I could still see it. It's so hard to put it into words but I knew that that gentleness, which ought to have made what it represented fragile and destroyable, did the exact opposite. That gentleness was . . . it must have been . . . supernatural, and because of that it made what it represented entirely indestructible. It also made it beyond what we understand as mundane human. Whatever I saw must have been from somewhere else, Joe and–'

'Oh?' I interrupted her bitterly in our beautiful antique-filled Lonning parlour on the second evening of her confession in the last weeks of 2007. 'And where would that be?'

'Heaven,' she said without a moment's hesitation. And then she blushed purple. 'I mean–'

'Oh I believe you,' I almost shouted. 'I mean it was uttered so spontaneously I can't but believe you believe it. It came out without any censor, just like in those Freudian word-association games.'

She trembled. 'Don't tell anyone, Joe, will you! Don't tell the world that your wife is . . .'

I said angrily: 'Having an affair in her early seventies? Or having a literal vision of Heaven in a village dance hall? Which one exactly should I keep mum about, Liz?'

She started crying which for some reason made me all the madder. Seventy-three-year-olds in tears can sometimes seem more embarrassingly worn and wearisome than poignantly beautiful.

She said, 'Both. But if you have to tell anyone you can tell them about my . . . what you call my affair. Which is no longer an affair as I've told you. It's all over and I've finished it, and all I want now is for you to forgive.'

4

Some verbs are much more important in our lives than others. For some it is to love, for others to eat or to fuck or to spend or to buy or to bully or to succeed or to conquer or to gamble or, in the case of the ill, to recover and/or live. In the case of the dialect there is one verb that behaves differently from all others, so radically different that one can only assume it must have been crucially significant when the Vikings first took foreign Cumbrian root. The verb is 'to take' and perhaps the stock image of the Viking pillaging everything that moved or didn't move wherever they went is not irrelevant here. In a nutshell, these picturesque bandits 'took' liberties by 'taking' everything they 'took' a fancy to, on the robust maxim, you do all the giving, subject Cumbrians, and we do all the bloody taking!

The dialect verb 'to take' is *ter tyan* where bizarrely *tyan* is the past participle form meaning 'taken'. Bearing in mind that English 'a' becomes dialect *ya*, 'taken' has become *tyaken*, a word which is never used, but only in its contracted form *tyan*. The next quaint linguistic stage is that *tyan* is used for *all forms* of the verb 'to take', even including some crazily invented, composite and artificial forms. Let me explain:

I take a liberty! *Ah tyan a lipperty!*

I took a stroll down High Street! *Ah tyan a gander doon Tie Strit!*

I will take an Alka-Seltzer! *Ah'll tyan an Alkie Salty!*

I will have to take a brand name aperient! *Ah'll hev ter tyan a douse ev Sirop ev Fix!*

Take a break, boon companion! (imperative) *Tyan a brekk, marra!*

So in dialect it's literally 'I *taken* a bus to Carlisle', 'I will *taken* a bus to Carlisle', 'I'll have to *taken* a bus', and imperative form '*Taken* a bus to Carlisle [if you wish to be eco-bloody-conscious]!' Add to that the artificial forms, *Ah's tyannin a bus ter Carel* (literally, 'I'm *takening* a bus to Carlisle') and *Ah's ganna tyan* ('I'm going to *taken*') and we are in the diametrically opposite world to the Eskimos who have ten thousand different words for snow. Instead we have a land of the hypnotised and subjugated where there is only *one* unvarying form of a vital verb whether it is intended as past, present, future, conditional, imperative or anything else. All forms, all tenses, are all stated and defined *in the past*, whether understood as near or remote.

Oh? So what does that mean, Mr I Spy Linguistics Made Easy For All?

That to the Cumbrians, past, present and future are *all the bloody same* and they are all in the bloody past! That the poor buggers have no sense of the wholly impenetrable and unintelligible and painfully uncontrollable future, because everything they know and understand is cast in the eternally bloody past and finished!

Mm. Well, I've heard worse theories to explain this provincial anomie and stagnance. And now that I am seventy-three, I feel, how shall I put it, just a little free to speak my candid opinion.

Mm. Let's get back to *Galluses Galore.*

Further instalment of *Galluses Galore*

Fenton Baggrow was sat in a Cumbrian pub in Howgill not far from Northumbrian Slaggyford, and was not just braces-free but impudently sporting a belt (*bare-fyasst impidence an owny a few mile frae law-apidin Slaggy*). It was not just any old belt either, it was an antique kid's snake belt from about 1960 which he'd managed to acquire on eBay for rather less than you might expect.

'eBay?' said his drinking companion, seventy-eight-year-old Jakie Tunstall, a rather ugly, bulky sheep farmer who even by 2018 had still not got round to acquiring a computer, much less going online. 'What would that be, Fenton? (*Wat the stimmin shite is sek as yon?*)'

Fenton briefly and with admirable lucidity explained about the internet shopping site. Jakie eventually understood it as being something like the old *Exchange and Mart* magazine, but without the fun of writing preliminary letters or telephoning someone down in say Stevenage or Wyre Piddle (*next till Pishy Trainride doon in Dosset*). Jakie, who in the 1950s was a pop fanatic, would anxiously ask them if they really did have the first 78 record by The Drifters, only to be told yes indeed they did as long as Tunstall didn't mind its vintage backside being a trifle scuffed.

It would help with narrative accuracy, not to say vividness, if we emphasised the following. During this exchange between the two Howgill drinkers, Fenton's interlocutor was wearing an extremely bulky overcoat and as a consequence the ends of his braces were looped around his ears. As a further consequence he had the braces at full extension, otherwise in stooping his neck towards the counter and his pint he might have struggled to get his lips there as quickly as he wished (*Tinsel bean an owd cuss ev seventy eight hed allus wore galluses anywez, but nooadays he mad shoor t'illastic wuss as lyeuss as posbel in cess his thussty gob got pullt awae frae his glass ev yal juss like summat oot ev Arald Hoyd er Max Henhut er Bucks Punny*). Nevertheless for all his meticulous forethought with the tensile setting of his braces, Tunstall was not exactly relaxed with his pint. This was not least because when he glanced in the pub mirror he saw this startled old hill farmer with a hernia truss contraption around his straining head. Though surprisingly, by the spring of 2018, a majority of the locals had learnt to put up with the grotesque sight of trussed up Michelin men, or alternatively chaps with elasticated ear rings that travelled mysteriously down to their hips only to be buried beneath their coats. They were growing used to their own absurdity and indignity to a certain extent, and therefore no longer fell about laughing when they saw an Ear Suspension Option looking as forlorn as a pet spaniel forced to wear a trilby hat to amuse its callous owner.

'You know what?' Tunstall said suddenly, pointing miserably at the loops around his ears. 'I thought I was getting used to these damn things. But seeing you wearing that nice little snake belt, I feel . . . I feel like a . . . like an idiot.'

Baggrow sank in a single swallow half a pint of unreal ale and replied with characteristic adamantine candour, 'You definitely look like an idiot. And there's only one practical solution, Jakie.'

Tunstall looked suspicious. 'Breaking the bloody law?'

'Take the bloody things off! (*Tyan t'buggers off!*) If the law is stupid, which it is, then it's your moral duty to disobey it (*an than he kwotit a laal bit ev an owd Lating motty that went strait ower Jakie's puzzelt eed*).'

Old Tunstall glanced about very uneasily. 'That's all very well. But you're the only bugger round here defying them! Everybody apart from a few show-off twenty-year-old kids has soon got shot of their belts. Those kids thought it was OK to prance past the special constables without any braces, but they were whisked off to court as soon as you like (*they got browt up in front ev sturn-fyasst Carel madgiestitts an that took t'smile frae their grinning fyasses. They're noo on curfoo aspos, an hess ter report till t'pleece ivvry bliddy day wearin speshul galluses markt wit a bliddy greet "ASAP" for "aunty soshal aktivitties punnyshment"*).'

Fenton talked about organised solidarity at that point,

and said that if all or even a significant number of Cumbrian males refused to wear braces, that would soon get the law repealed. Not a single pilot-scheme male was able to confirm that the wearing of braces did what the premier (*t'top gadger*) said it would do, i.e. miraculously firm up their citizenship skills and all-round moral fibre. How the hell scoffed Fenton could sporting daft old galluses teach genuine moral values, and likewise how could wearing a belt, snake or not, supposedly foster slyness, deviance, rebellion and sloth? It was all of a piece (*aw ev a piss*), he went on angrily, with this recent draconian legislation that penalised folk who were overweight or to use the daunting new technical term 'obese' (*awpiss*). All this was on top of the ground-breaking decade-long investigation into the overall health of the British nation, which was obviously going to lead to a *compulsory* dietary intake of five pieces of fresh fruit or vegetable a day (*wedder thoo's awpiss er bliddy nut, tho hess ter eat five pisses ev sek as orrinsh, appel, sangsummer, cabbish, er hattychoke er sparragarse if thoo's edikatit an weel heelt*).

Tunstall sighed and said he had an enormously stout female cousin called Aggie Mary who had recently been refused varicose vein hospital treatment in nearby Haltwhistle (*Halty*) on account of her glaring obesity (*owd Aggie Merry's bare-fyasst awpissity*). Given that Haltwhistle was famous as the exact geographical centre of Britain, surely, added Jakie mournfully, it might also have decided to be a second geographical centre for showing tolerance towards the circulatory problems of the porky and the corpulent.

'And while we're at it,' interpolated Fenton with a mordant look on his face, 'the schoolkids are being mercilessly persecuted as well these days (*ee sez t'poor laal schyeul-bairns carn't stuff theirsels neah mare wit Mosty Munch er Malty Sirs er Cadpies Flyaks oot ev t'fendin mashins! Instead they ev ter shuffel five pisses ev cabbish, orrinsh,*

70

peer, pitch, blackites, collyphoo, sproots, lets, brockholey an udder dammt coo fodder inter their mooths ivvry bliddy day.)'

So saying he unwrapped and masticated his fourth Mars Bar of the day and alongside that his seventeenth packet of Worcester sauce crisps. These were the only foodstuffs anyone ever saw him eat, and given that diet and all round well being are supposed to be related, his phenomenal homespun learning, intellectual and emotional independence etc. would seem to be a living testimony to these murky comestibles (*Mash Bass an Whoosher Krishps ed likely given im aw them greet brains and greet big woods, nut ter speak ev Baggra's amyazin gift fer bonny motts, aunty climax, hyperbollicks, sinkeydonkey an sek like*).

'Look at me!' intoned Fenton suddenly and with a determinedly didactic tone to his voice. 'I don't believe in any old-fashioned values! I don't believe in the bloody work ethic, or in social responsibility (*wat t'ya time top body Madgie Thunder allus wantit, even if she dint believe fer a minnit there wuss sek a bliddy thing as "sosighty"*). I spend all day and every day drinking like a fish, and if I'm not doing that I'm biking from one pub to the next or I'm at home pissing about eating Worcester sauce crisps and reading interesting books.'

'Aye,' grunted Tunstall. 'You're a damn bliddy queer un.' (*An he sez bi way ev parenthissis, wat ah want ter know is where in cussin ell duss thoo git aw this brass frae?*)

Baggrow smiled and gave that teasing look that infuriated those acquaintances of his who worked and toiled like dogs on the fellsides, in the factories, on the farms and occasionally as postmen or gas-meter readers.

'I live on fresh air (*on swit bugger aw*),' he said. 'And it drives folk mad wanting to know just how the hell how I do it! Worse than that, I drink twenty odd pints a day which in 2018 sets me back a hundred quid, but I never ever get drunk (*nut even a mottycombe*). And if the police ever stop me on my bike and breathalyse me, the breathalyser says I'm as sober as a . . . as a . . .'

'Judge?' supplied Tunstall.

'You're joking! As a badger.'

'Exactly,' expostulated Jakie suddenly very angry. 'As well as defying the braces law and common sense, you defy bloody old science.'

At that Baggrow snorted and said something elliptical and theoretical which poor old Tunstall failed to grasp (*cos ee sez that t'pull ev grafty, hentrippy, an sum udder law ev turmidynamicks, is tree things ah can easy tyan, er dyeuh widoot, Jakie*).

Old Tunstall beseeched him: 'You don't make any income, Fenton, and we've all been spying on you for years and years, and you definitely don't live on benefits or handouts. You drink oceans of strong ale (*Tinsel rackt iss brens fer lifely cumparisen, and sez t'syam vollum as t'Deed See, t'Reid See, t'Casper See an mare ev gey fierce yal*) but you never ever get drunk! The queer thing is that every single bugger in the county (*as weel as t'Scuttish Howm, an Notumlan Halty, Lumley an Slaggy an mare*) loves you to bits, even though you're a terrible man. Even though you never ever stir a bat! You're supposed by law these days to prove you're a good and loyal citizen, but you piss on all of that, Fenton Baggrow, as if it's just one bloody big joke.'

'Let's put it this way,' adumbrated Baggrow. 'Citizenship aside, I don't go around doing anyone a good turn, except when I *talk* to them. Manners cost me nothing and I'm friendly, Jakie, I'm everybody's pal and I'm nobody's enemy, apart from the authorities. I listen to folk, have you noticed (*even them wat's leet as caff, even them fwoaks wit slates lyeuss wat twoaks away an chunters till theirsels*)? Everybody in this world wants to be listened to, isn't that a fact? But such as Thomas Purley, the premier (*t'top gadger, Tommy Pullet*) he might believe in citizenship skills (*t'owd skills ev citiesinshit*) but he doesn't want to listen to folk.

Instead he wants folk to listen to him! He wants folk to listen till it hurts! He wants them to listen till it bleeds! He wants them to eat at least five pieces (*fife bliddy pisses*) of fresh fruit and vegetables and not stuff their kites with Milky Ways and UmBongo! He wants them to be stout citizens, but not obese ones! So far he's only refusing fat folk like cousin Aggie Mary their hospital operations, but before long it'll be either a fine or a jail sentence for being more than fourteen stone (yah mare *oonce, an thoo's weel an treuly fyeukt*).'

Tunstall worriedly asked him what was to be done, even though like everyone who lacks that old-fashioned thing called courage, he already knew the answer. Baggrow told him that what was needed was indeed personal courage: meaning independent-mindedness and a strong sense of personal liberty, just as the old French revolutionaries had demanded. Even though, added Fenton with a sigh, they had made a bloody mess of it, had been far too bloody about it altogether (*Fenten sez Rubberspit, Dante an them udder owd highdelistick Frenshie marraboys aw went a bit ower far in tryin ter preuf a point agyanst t'Hongsyhong Resin*). So this time round, in 2018 in revolutionary Cumbria, no spilling of blood, that was essential (*a sinky kwa nin*)! But likewise no more of those idiotic galluses tight around the poor old brainbox, no more compulsory five pieces, however easy, and no prospect of being arrested and fined or put in Durham or Haverigg clink for being fourteen stone one ounce!

Tunstall, old as he was and ugly as he was, felt very roused by this insurrectionary dialectic. He wanted to go out and smash a few faces which was how he used to behave once or twice as an overworked and underpaid young farmhand addicted to the music of The Drifters back in 1957 (*wen ee wuss pisht up ev a Satdy neet sixty 'ear sen at a Yung Fammer's do at Langtoon er Brampten er Halty, an ee'd gah lyeukin ter bray t'fyass off t'fust feller ee met*). He put this as a serious strategy to Fenton Baggrow now. Let them go out and batter a few folk at random in say Carlisle and hope it changed things for the better or the worse, and with a heartening fifty per cent chance of the former! Fenton smiled at him indulgently. He said to the Howgill farmer who was twice his age that evidently (*wurds till t'effect*) sagacious sapience and the possession of white hairs were not invariable correlates.

'Aye,' snapped Jakie very impatiently. 'But what should we *do* Fenton? I don't care what it is you want me to do, no matter how desperate or dangerous! I'm your man! (*An Tinsel gahs on ter brag, thoo's sturt mi owd eroic Noth Penning bluid wid thee flaysome plitical rapple-roozin! Till ah's gurt insindery an kwit irrashnal, Fenten!*)

Baggrow then made a gesture of whispering into his companion's ear. And it was not just any old public-house ear of course. It was peculiarly uncomfortable because of the braces loop wrapped tight about it which meant it was inclined at a strained torque of about thirty degrees, a bit like a paper animal's ear as fashioned by origami. Nor was Tunstall's put-upon left lug particularly enjoying the astringent aftermath of twelve pints of light ale mingled with melted chocolate and chemically manufactured Worcester sauce.

Fenton confided something at great length and in considerable detail into that straining lughole. Whereupon Tunstall, who was old enough to think he had heard everything outlandish and outrageous in his day, turned as white as a sheet.

'Fugg me stiff! Fugg me gently! Fugg me sideways!' he objurgated coarsely though not without a certain natural musical rhythm. And he remained in a state of frozen shock for the next two minutes. At last he muttered hoarsely:

'You're not just mad, son, you're bloody lethal! You can't do that, Fenton. You can't do what you say you're going to do.'

Fenton was amused by the old man's terrible pallor which was slowly changing into a bilious shade of livid green. Tunstall stammered mortified: 'It's not just breaking the law, it's . . . man, they'll sling you in jug and chuck away the bloody key (*t'owd wassacomie convenshun on Yooman Rites'll be skopt oot ev t'winder as syeun as thoo bliddy well likes*)!

Baggrow grinned. 'I'll get away with it, you'll see. I have ways and means. Don't you worry.'

But Tunstall was not just anxious about Baggrow's personal safety. 'Hang on. You've told me all about it and in a hell of a lot of detail. That means I'm a thingummy, doings, damn, what's the damn word, something to do with bastard bike shops?'

Baggrow knew at once what he was on about. 'An accessory (*an owdcussery*), Jakie?

After some frantic thought, Tunstall eventually gave a queer little smirk of relief. Then to Baggrow's surprise he took on an expression of incomparable slyness. 'So how d'you know I won't tell on you (*an Fenten cud see owd Tinsel wuss coshitatin, ah'll mebbe even git a guffment boonty ev ten thoosan pun fer rattin on this mad yung bugger!*)?'

Fenton had earlier inflated an empty crisp bag and he suddenly exploded it between his palms which had both an immediate and an associative effect on Jakie. The old man shook so hard with the shock that his braces elastics shot loose from his lugs and went flying down to deal him a fearful and symmetrical twin buffet across both teats (*Jakie vanya shit yeller leetnin wen t'krishp pakit expludit! Ee gev sek a shakk that t'galluses lyeups floo lyeuss an clattert im across byath tits like a pair ev ellish thunnerpolts*).

Fenton glared at his now timid and very pliant companion. He asked him in an icy voice if he had ever read Charles Dickens's *Great Expectations* (*Chas Dixon's 'Ivvry-thin's Ganna Bi Juss Champion'*). When Tunstall looked uncomprehending, he persisted, OK, had he seen any of the umpteen films or TV series had been made of the immortal classic in the last seventy or eighty years? At last Jakie stuttered that he had seen one on telly about 1961, and he made hasty reference to Mrs Joe and Tickler with a nervous and insincere guffaw. Baggrow then mentioned the escaped convict Magwitch who had threatened the boy Pip with dreadful things should he tell on him. One of the terrible things was this mysteriously horrible and ubiquitous friend of his, the hideous young man, who would seek Pip out no matter where he was and when, day or night, door locked or unlocked . . .

Even dopey Tunstall got the drift, and he paled and shook yet again. Baggrow pointed out that just as he could magically live on fresh air and subsist on infinite quantities of chocolate and crisps and ale without getting sick or drunk . . . so he could magically find out traitorous Tunstall no matter where he was hiding! Should he dare, that is, to go and blab like a fool about this revolutionary plan! Tunstall was the only person Baggrow had told of his intentions, so if word got out it could only be he was the perfidious leaking vessel.

'Agreed?' said Baggrow poking Tunstall painfully on both his wounded tits.

Tunstall nodded obsequiously and offered hastily to buy the next round (*an freetent Tinsel thowt till issel, ah divent wannt sumbody like Herbert Mad Witch's orrible marra stickin is turrible greet fyass agyanst mi bedroom winder at fower o'clock in t'mornin! Ah wad fill me breeks wit t'shock, an than they'd tyan mi awae till t'Owd Fwoaks Yam in Penrith an makk us eat five pisses a day ev bliddy piss an crats an collyphoo an prud pins an rungy pins an putty pins an . . .*)

End of instalment of *Galluses Galore*

It was the night after the Greek banquet and we were in The Lonning lounge discoursing as in an Aldous Huxley novel about the relationship between epistemology, metaphysics and pragmatism . . . no we weren't, certainly not, that is a Cummerlan Tyal-style lie . . . we were talking about the best way to cook fennel, the exquisite vegetable that is as opposed to the lustrous herb. Liz had just gone out to her Greek For Business and Pleasure night class in Carlisle, and had insisted on giving me the mobile number of the teacher Mrs Papadopoulos, to prove she was there trying to pronounce *ftani* and *vdhomadha* and not still committing adultery. I believed her of course while still feeling anxious for the future, not to speak of the troublous present and the trying past. And this at seventy-three mind you, when your troubles are only supposed to be of the bowels, the brain functions and the bastards who would have you show them your will in advance and have you put away in a residential home merely for allowing your mouth to drop open on occasion.

I didn't know any Greek recipes for fennel, but Marjorie Staff who was a globe-trotting journalist in her past life described a variety of Italian salads, including one with oranges, fennel, olives, tomatoes and extra virgin, which I shall no doubt attempt one of these days. Cora Dorr knew about everyone's favourite, *finocchi siciliana*, the braised fennel topped with strong cheese and black olives and put under the grill. Neither Pargeter and his Harley Davidson nor Dixon the lay reader had ever tasted fennel, so I told them about that pasta sauce where the vegetable is grated and stewed along with lemon juice and rind and mixed with cream and a little sugar. Once tipped over the pasta, the sauce is decorated with fried pistachios and most people who have consumed it express a wish to pass away on the spot as there cannot possibly be an experience to match it in simultaneous sensual expansiveness and gustatory focus for the next three or four thousand decades . . .

'And while we're at it,' I said, on my third or it might have been sixth glass of Kourtaki, 'I don't usually give away every last trade secret, only nine tenths. But I take a delight in imparting recipes that are both gourmet and child's play to do. Isn't that a startling idea, by the way, something that is virtuoso but *easy*? Luckily for all of us the combination is rare in all fields of life not just cookery.'

'Why luckily?' mumbled Pargeter who had eaten the best part of a kilo jar of preserved cherries I had brought back from Milos. 'Wouldn't it be great for all concerned if everything in cookery was a piece of piss?'

Instantly he blushed as his eyes met first very old Marjorie's and then lay reader William Dixon's.

Marjorie sighed and said, 'I may be very old and very posh but it really doesn't exclude me from the most basic and indispensable vocabulary. How could I have possibly functioned as a roving journalist if I hadn't learnt how to cope with frightening situations by learning how to swear. I really don't flinch at the word piss, you know. I use it quite often, along with fuck, shit, balls and ballocks. There's only one swear word I'm not sure about these days. There has been this recent reassessment on ideological feminist grounds of the word cun–'

William Dixon stared at some honey on a preserved quince and blurted, 'I think it depends very much on the manner in which the words are uttered. I certainly don't object to an expressive, harmless metaphor like "piece of piss".'

'The reason,' I blurted impatiently, 'why it's not a good thing for excellence to come easy, is that it would mean your Beethovens, George Eliots, Miles Davises, Katherine Mansfields etc. would be growing on trees and frankly that would be unmitigated hell. Genius would be debased and no one would ever know shit from sugar . . . sorry, Marjorie, sorry, parson. Excellence is surely a combination of phenomenal hard graft and long experience, on top of any native talent. But now and again, at least in cooking, and it is rather mind-boggling, you find something that is amazing and that any bloody fool could make with his eyes shut.'

'Explain,' said Cora Dorr.

Marjorie said, 'French toast with syrup is a good example. Thirty odd years ago it was a middle-class addiction in all the cafés and stalls in New Delhi. That and milky coffee was what all the better-off young professionals guzzled. In Calcutta it was different, it was blinking chips of all things, English-style chips with tomato sauce served in little metal bowls.'

'No,' I objected, 'we're talking about fennel not about eggy bloody toast. Here's how to do it and you can tell your friends it's your own invention. Just take the fennel bulb and cut out and discard, the dross, the fibrous root and those celery-style projections at the top. Chop coarsely what's left and put it in a carrier bag . . .'

I paused. They were sat there like expectant pups waiting for the stick to be thrown.

'Then throw away the carrier bag.'

'Eh?' said Pargeter. 'But what's . . . ?'

'Only joking. No, inside the carrier bag you have a couple of tablespoons of plain flour. Shake your coarsely chopped fennel vigorously inside the bag to get it evenly coated with the flour.'

Marjorie Staff said, 'Emitting a sinuous Edmundo Ros rumba numba while you are shaking.'

'Precisely. Then take out all the bits of floured fennel and put them in a large frying pan and fry them in good olive oil slowly, for as long as you like. They will turn brown and soft and succulent and if you serve them garnished with the little bits of feathery herb you have kept from the original bulb . . .'

Cora Dorr said, 'You will hypnotise your friends and keep the jaws of your ugly foes well occupied. That would also be an impressive starter in my opinion. Pitta bread and yoghurt and salad alongside.'

'It is virtuoso cooking but so simple even a Full English breakfast addict could make it. Bit by bit he or she could be weaned away from hideous meat, and bit by bit . . .'

Pargeter finally couldn't restrain himself. 'It's a bit late in the day, but I really need to know this. Why don't you eat meat? What is it you've got against it? I've never eaten better food in my life than yours but . . .'

I said, 'No need to be embarrassed. It's a fair question. Guess?'

Cora Dorr stared up at my seventeenth-century oak beams for a while and opined, 'Religious reasons.'

William Dixon looked extremely serious and said, 'It might be out of turn to say this, but I believe Mr Gladstone, sorry, I mean Joe here, for all his good-natured vehemence and humorous abrasiveness and so on, is very likely a deeply spiritual person.'

That killed the conversation for the best part of half a minute whereupon I answered: 'I really wish that I was.'

What I really wanted to say at that juncture was that my wife, who I subsequently learnt had been conjugating the verb *thelo*, I want, I desire, down in Carlisle, had had the actual goods, the real experience, not just the blether and the talk about it. All that in the context of an embarkation on a protracted sinful act, the breaking of a hallowed commandment. Later, even more ironically, in the same village dance hall, there had been a second apparently numinous experience which would seem to have confuted or at least contradicted the first. But I will come to all of that in good time . . .

'You don't like killing animals,' said Marjorie Staff. 'No, I don't mean that at all. Amend to "don't like the killing of". That's why I'm a life-long vegetarian at any rate.'

Pargeter said, 'Is that why you are, Joe? Are you a life-long vegetarian?'

'Yes and no,' I said. 'I don't like the killing of animals, and that is why I'm a vegetarian. No, I am not a life-long abstainer. I ate meat with great gusto and with the best of them until my early thirties. And no it isn't for religious reasons unless the feelings I have about killing animals could be described as unconsciously religious.'

Cora Dorr said, 'I ate meat by the barrowload until seven years ago. Then in 2001 we had that unbelievable foot and mouth plague. I saw all those tragic mounds of sheep and cattle carcasses burning away night after night on the television screen. I know there's no comparison but the only thing I could compare those pyres and trenches to was the old newsreels of extermination camps with the bulldozers shovelling up the corpses. I saw all those farmers weeping like stricken children when their prize herds were butchered, sometimes by freelance slaughterers from hundreds of miles away. The thing about those mountains of dead sheep was they looked so . . . incredibly blameless. They had never harmed anybody or anything and there they were piled up in those disgusting hills of corpses. They actually radiated something . . . a kind of sadness and a kind of warning I don't know. After two weeks of it I went out and bought five vegetarian recipe books and I've never once looked back.'

I said, 'There are about five thousand variables relevant to the discussion but let's just consider four thousand. The foot and mouth evil was a function of the alienated and unfeeling vileness of the meat industry which is inherent and integral to its smooth running. All meat eaters are complicit in that vileness as they have to shoulder responsibility for this thing they insist on having at all costs. There has to be *cheap* meat, not just meat, for the consumer, and cheap meat means as far as the animal is concerned you can do what you fucking well like, I'm sorry parson.'

William Dixon blushed. 'It sounds like honest anger. Possibly not righteous anger, but . . .'

'Cheap meat can only possibly be got by the cruelty of the conveyor, by turning a blind eye and by the cutting of all humane corners. The producer has to pretend that the evil things he is doing are not evil things, and if you are a meat eater you have to blank out the truth that you are the end of the chain that is evil, as you tuck into your succulent pie or your exquisite sausage.'

Pargeter wasn't keen on being told he was complicit in evil and he even stopped shovelling down the preserved Milos cherries.

'Sooner or later one of the suppliers, the sourcers of the cheap meat, will turn out to be either a crook or an imbecile or both . . . and he or she will be feeding their beasts a swill that is rampant and crawling with microbes. It is the logical terminal stage of not caring, and wishing to make a fuck-you-all living at all costs. Quite reasonably the buggers doing the dirtiest of the dirty work are thinking, you all eat meat, you all want it cheap, you're all torturing these calves, chickens and turkeys as much as I bloody am. The 2001 foot and mouth plague was therefore not a one-off anomaly, nor an accident waiting to happen. The true miracle is that these or similar plagues are not bursting out all over the country once a week.'

Marjorie Staff said, 'There is that kind of argument and there is also the anecdotal one. About twenty years ago, Mr Pargeter, I was travelling in the Dodecanese on my way back from Turkey and I stopped off at an island so small I can't even remember its name.'

I asked with some excitement, 'Lipsi? Arki? Agathonisi?'

'No, it wasn't any of those. No matter, it was very very tiny and it got about ten tourists a year I believe. But it had a hora, a village capital like they all do, stuck up on a not very steep hill for ancient defensive purposes. The hora, which was blindingly white, had one long street of about fifty houses and a very old church and that was it. At the far end of the street and at the top of the hill, I stopped for a breather and to look down on the bay below. It was early evening, about seven o' clock. There was the serenest stillest twilight which can only be experienced in Greece, nowhere else, a kind of benign and eternal stillness. There were bright red flowers potted in olive-oil tins and their scent was very tender and was mixed with some scent of herbs from the scrubland above the houses. I think it was oregano which is my favourite herb.'

'Mine too,' I sighed. 'All else are equal last.'

'Anyway, right at the top of the village there was a kind of outhouse inside a little sheltered yard. I looked over the wall and inside the outhouse, which had a roof and a couple of supporting posts but no doors as far as I recall, were some pigs.'

'I see,' I said. 'And the Greeks certainly love to consume their pork, their *khirino*.'

'They were extremely handsome animals. They were not a kind of pig I have ever seen before. They were not the classic British obese porker, which I'm sure has as much feeling and sensitivity as any other animal but which outwardly at least does not seem too subtle. They were big of course these Greek pigs, but not gross and not comical, and they had rust-coloured bristles of hair on them and they had very, how can I put it, quite intolerably expressive eyes.'

'Ah,' I said, feeling a little odd. 'I can well believe.'

'It was the combination of a perfect twilight, a tiny remote island that rarely saw tourists, and the sight of those four beautiful pigs that didn't really look like pigs that gradually and definitely . . . unnerved me. No, that's the wrong word. I felt such a strength and mixture of very powerful and very disconcerting feelings. They had about them, these pigs, what I can only call an extraordinary modesty, their eyes had a terrible modesty and an effect or emanation of something I hesitate to call grace . . . I'm sorry, William, to be using words like those before a priest.'

Dixon said very carefully, 'It was God the Creator who made your Greek pigs. I'm sure he knew precisely what he was doing.'

'You think so?' asked the ninety-five-year-old in the same voice as a wondering five-year-old.

'I am cast-iron certain.'

'There was such a poetry and significance in their eyes. I felt so intrusive as if I had no right to trespass so blatantly where they were, poking my posh and ugly old English nose over their little island wall. I forgot to say they were lit up by the evening twilight which made them look even more special and as if in some frieze or tableau. There was absolutely nobody around except myself and the pigs. This is what I'm trying to get at . . . as well as a secret grace, there was something else those Greek animals had. There are other special and accurate words to describe those remote island animals, but I genuinely don't think the words have been born or uttered by anyone yet. I felt that their little sunlit yard and wide open sty was their special domain and that in a moral and even legal sense, they owned it, not the farmer or smallholder. Perhaps the most important thing is that as soon as I saw them I knew in the way a child would painfully realise that they were meant for killing, they weren't there as pets. Handsome and exceptional creatures that they were, they were bound to end up being butchered and going down people's necks. Their beauty and that unchangeable fact were inseparable and I wished like a small child that the world was different and beautiful animals weren't killed. I also felt that they knew on every level their fate as well as I did, and that they lived with that and that their poetry as animals was a tacit accusation against our species which is an unrepentant expert at killing anything and everything that is beautiful.'

5

My benefactor Uncle Harrison began smoking cigarettes at the age of three, so he reckoned, and continued the habit into sanguine old age. He was the youngest of ten children, all boys, and he told me that everything in his family followed a kind of rolling domino trajectory from oldest to youngest sibling. All the sarks and keitels meaning all the shirts and rough jackets were passed down from father to eldest Harold and thence via Jim, Arnold, Thomas, Willy and the four youngest uncles including my father and all the way to Harrison . . . with the words, *ere thoo is Arald/ Jim/Arnal/Tommas/Willy . . . Arrison, it's thy turrn noo, tyan ho'd ev this.* Likewise when all ten sons were working or idling in the rainy fields at the far-flung ends of Bewcastle or Bailey, the same Woodbine would go via nine pairs of filial lips until the dog-end reached infant Harrison, who could not on grounds of strict moral equity be left out of the clan sequence, even if his first puff had him coughing his three-year-old lungs out. (Dog-end by the way, and forgive me the hasty brackets, is a 2 fit only for a 1, assuming that is, all else being imaginatively equal, that a dog could happily be a fag smoker.)

Contrast the primitive 1924 North Cumbrian anthropology of Harrison's hand-me-down sarks and fags with my son Desmond's 2008 variant down in prosperous market town Wilts. Desmond, who is of course Harrison's great-nephew, took over his job of arts-centre manager having moved sideways in local government from the accounts department where though young and able he was not as yet obviously destined for senior management. There had been very few applications for the post and those they'd looked at were either far too young and woefully outré in their ambitions (weekend international poetry marathons, short experimental films from Macedonia, improvised atonal jazz performances, etc.) or had had far too many years in similar posts where not only had they clearly ossified to an impressive degree but would also demand the appropriate salary. Desmond expressed a wish to take on the ailing post, even though he had no previous experience and was not qualified in arts administration. His local government supremos showed a certain heavy surliness at his dogged confidence that he could not only make something of the post, but also make it run at a profit or rather not, as hitherto, at an embarrassing loss. He was taken on reluctantly on a six-month probationary period, and told he would be whanged back to accounts faster than the speed of light if and when, and the latter was much the likelier in their view, he made an arse/balls/cock-up/pig's ear of it.

A non-bracketed parenthesis here. Pig's ear is obviously ext. as messy as a 2 of 1. But as for cock-up? I'm not sure I dare think about it much less articulate or write it. Parse it yourself if you are so darn cocky (ha!), and I hope you come out with something connected to blameless prize poultry exhibits. But all that aside, Desmond Gladstone took them all by surprise, because he went in there like, to continue the farmyard similes, a bull at a gate, and like the no-nonsense pragmatist he is gave the Wilts market town punters exactly what they wanted even if until Desmond arrived the buggers had no idea what that was.

Desmond, as well as following his own hunches, had been doing intensive background research. He had spent a whole fortnight ringing up arts managers in small market towns all over the British Isles and had been guilelessly frank about picking their brains for successful audience-pullers. After about a hundred and fifty phone calls and totting up his common factor ticklists he had deduced that there were two things above all others that got the English, Scottish, Welsh and Northern Irish market town public into their arts-centres in droves. Subsequently three months into his probationary period he was already gaining capacity audiences as the formula that he had evolved was seemingly impregnable, the Wiltshire arts-patronising populace could simply not get enough of it.

The formula, such as it was, was two-fold (ext. that is 2 into 1 or ext. having 1 of 2s?). Only two items from Desmond's telephone research were cast-iron guaranteed (ext. 2 as enduring as 1, 1 itself being a 2 that is 1?) to win big audiences, and also command a hefty ticket price. I wonder if you can guess what those two things were. The Royal Shakespeare Company and the Hallé Orchestra? Ken Dodd and Ben Elton? Yes, up to a point, a huge name and a huge reputation, especially one with five decades or more performing experience behind it, is always going to be a winner. Unfortunately some of these illustrious acts charged the earth and their ticket prices were astronomical. They could logically only be had once in a while so what in the meantime was to be the small-town arts-centre bread and butter?

Two-fold as I said. The first fold, to give you a clue, rests on the childlike addiction a great many humans have to the miracle of mimesis. And no, I don't mean performing impressionists which Desmond soon found out might work once if it was a superstar catch like Rory Bremner, but otherwise the lesser fry would lose him a packet. The mimesis we are talking about is *tribute bands* of which after five years in post Desmond has hired no less than a hundred, some of them several times, to fill to the gills his gleaming steel and glass arts venue. The other, before I lose my thread and get lost in the wonder of words and concepts like 'tribute' and 'mimesis' is, and it pains me to say it, I have to hold the abhorrent word between mile-long fire-tongs is . . . clairvoyance.

This second item amounts to vicarious cheap thrills, does it not, a two-bit cheapskate flutter with the inscrutable beyond and the tantalising supernatural? Most of it, I'm sure you would concede, is not about offering necessary assistance, however compromised and however notionally harmless, to the bereaved and the grief-stricken, but about 'reading' people's minds. As for this reading, for it to be successful, the more general and of a severely skim nature it is, the better and happier for all concerned. In this connection, at the age of seventy-three and having knocked about a bit all over the world, I can confirm you in what you already know in your heart of hearts . . . you would be more profitably employed in watching the downstairs sink emptying than in trying to penetrate another's mind, as most folks' so-called minds really aren't worth protracted scrutiny . . .

Why am I telling you all of this? Because I am annoyed, possibly even ashamed, that my son succeeds in life by giving his public a combination of plagiarism and frequent charlatanism. He doesn't give them Terence Rattigan or Samuel Beckett, not because these chaps ask hard questions and pose this terrible thing called poignance: he eschews them because, no matter how he dresses them up, the Wilts punters will eschew them first and he will lose his local government employers a sizeable quantity of money.

I am also telling you this because my son makes a handsome living and his envious father does not. He has a lecturer wife Deirdre and two brainy teenage children Sean and Madeleine and unless I am much deceived it is a stable family life and will always be so. I have not told him about his septuagenarian mother's recent affair nor assuredly has Liz. I think he would divorce the pair of us if we did tell him: Liz for the unutterably repugnant crime of combining old age with sex, and me for being so pathetic as a father and a husband that she could in theory, given her age and the strain of the loss-making Lonning guest house, be excused.

Desmond and I had one hell of a row the week after Liz told me all about Patrick. He was up visiting us on his own, or rather stopping off two nights en route to Edinburgh where he was convenor and principal speaker at some arts-managers' shindig. We were sat in our private sitting room rather than the guest lounge, old mother and old father and middle-years son, the first two smarting over recently revealed and painful knowledge. Desmond was talking entertainingly about his job, rather too amusingly as it happened. You could say he was being inordinately irrepressible and I even got it into my head that he knew something was terribly wrong between his parents and was rubbing it in for good measure. In retrospect of course that is highly unlikely as whatever he thinks of my erratic behaviour he dotes on Liz and always has done.

'Would you credit,' he said suddenly with a large glass of vintage port in his hand, 'that there are reckoned to be some five hundred Beatles tribute bands performing day in day out all over the world? At any one time "She Loves You, Yeah Yeah" is being sung in imitation Scouse by startlingly lifelike doubles in twenty or thirty countries simultaneously. It must be damn hard singing imitation Scouse if you're from Uruguay or the Maldives. I can hardly do it myself, can you Dad? Isn't that mind-blowing? As for Jimi Hendrix, who has been dead nearly forty years, in the UK alone there are at least a dozen tributes making a tolerable living, a much bigger number in France, an even bigger number in Germany, and an unbelievable profusion of Jimi take-offs in Japan.'

He went on to explain how the British Jimi bands tended to take root and flourish disproportionately in towns that were pleasingly assonant with the name Hendrix. In effect it wasn't just the lookalikes and singalikes that were enchanting the mesmerised audience, but the urban venue itself took a vicarious and magical part in the mimesis. Hence there was a riproaring London tribute band called Jimi Hendon, as well as a slightly less whirlwind Jimi Helmsley from sedate North Yorks and a passably rumbustious Jimi Heckmondwike from unsedate West Yorks. Further afield the guitar-string masticating Jimi Helsinki was justly world-renowned even though the drummer's and bass player's surnames were Ari Haanpaa and Gus Sillanpaa respectively. No, he said rather tersely to my jovial query, there wasn't a Jimi Heligoland as Heligoland wasn't a town, it was an amorphous area and amorphous areas could not claim partisan possession of a rock star with a similar name. But again at any one time in Tallinn, Taipei, Tokyo and fifty other vibrant cities there were umpteen clones of the one and only Jimi singing 'All Along The Watchtower', 'Are You Experienced?', or 'Manic Depression' while their drummers and bassists called Visnapuu, Wong and Watanabe were battering and beating away with all their cosmopolitan might. What's more, said Desmond, the unthinkable but in retrospect predictable was becoming more and more a regular phenomenon, at least on the provincial UK scene. This grotesque inversion of the musical cart before the musical horse was causing even arts manager Desmond Gladstone to have some vertiginous reflections on trifling things like identity, originality and who it was should have priority, the template or the copy?

'It's a baffling sort of situation,' he said, 'but some of the bands that are tributes to originals who are still performing, are actually more popular and make more money than the ones who gave them their living in the first place.'

He listed at that point sundry Swinging Sixties tribute bands called The Sneakers, the Sunny Bums, The Peacemakers and Peter and the Permits who charged up to seven hundred and fifty quid for a two-hour set of immaculate plagiarism while their now aging, bald or bedandruffed prototypes who could only be themselves and nothing else (and where was the skill in *that*?) would settle for three hundred and two free drinks and their knackered old Dormobile's petrol money.

I clapped my hands in confirmatory glee. 'Your tribute band wheel coming full circle underlines what has long been self-evident, Desmond. The modern 2008 UK not only prefers the ersatz to the real, it is prepared to put its money where its fakery-worshipping mouth is. The real you see is inevitably vulnerable and changing and thoroughly human, whereas the ersatz is like a machine on permanent hire, completely tireless and will never wear out until death or the nuclear bomb supervenes. The real musician, however objectively hopeless, needs this thing called inspiration to create, whereas the tribute parrot or canary only warbles and squawks and does imitative anatomical tics from parodic memory. And I would bet my shirt,' I added, at this point still in affable rather than combative mood, 'that the tribute chappies are not all paragons of modesty now that they are outselling and outstripping their originals.'

'Far from it,' sighed my son. 'A squabble broke out last month between the Peter and the Permits drummer and a shabby old tramp in the audience who claimed he had been third replacement for the original Sixties band forty-five years earlier. The old chap bawled out in between two numbers, "Where would you be if it wasn't for the likes of me, you wouldn't exist would you, you'd have nothing to fuckin imitate!" Whereupon the Permits' drummer bawled back, "The only reason you lot are remembered at all is because we keep your memory alive, you boozy old dosser! You need us more than we need you, I can effin well assure you." Then he went on to insinuate that P and the Ps were actually infinitely better than the amateurs they copied, which really got the old guy frothing at the mouth. God knows if he really was one of the original drummers, it might just have been his mania. I had to get the stewards to evict him he was so disruptive . . . but I gave him a tenner and said I could see his point of view.'

'So can I,' said Liz who if only for Desmond's sake was doing her best to rally from our marital misery. 'Tell me, don't these tribute lookalikes have very severe identity problems? I mean a film star's or a president's double only has very occasional duties, whereas these blokes who do their best to look like Mick Jagger or these women who are clones of Lulu or Cilla are performing night after night, aren't they? By the end of it don't they wonder who the hell they *really* are?'

'Yes,' said Desmond ruminatively. 'About a year ago I was witness to something extraordinary in that respect. I overheard a very able tribute Buddy Holly who was actually called Lance from Rawtenstall talking by a rare fluke to a childhood acquaintance of the real Buddy Holly. This friend of the real Buddy happened to be holidaying with his Wiltshire relatives and he couldn't resist going along to see his childhood pal being represented by a lookalike Lancastrian in his twenties called Lance. The American was actually very courteous and generous about Lance's flawless performance, but Lance was oddly patronising to his idol's real-life pal.'

Liz said, 'I can understand that. Rawtenstall Lance is thinking to himself, you knew the real one and with the best will in the world you must be aware that I'm not really him. You make me aware of my own flagrant and unsettling spuriousness.'

'I suppose so,' said Desmond. 'What he actually said to this blameless Yankee chap was, "It disturbs me to meet you, you know, because as far as I'm concerned I *am* Buddy and I don't recognise you as one of my childhood friends." The poor little American reasonably enough flinched at that, and after a longish pause that Lance did nothing to fill asked ever so politely for clarification. He eventually confirmed that Lance wasn't a deluded schizo-phrenic and didn't really believe himself to be either an original or a reincarnation. Lance was non-committal but very complex and metaphysical on that score. No he didn't mean he was literally someone else in the sense of being the real Buddy. What he seemed to be saying, and he'd been drinking a lot and was rather incoherent, was that his imitation was so authentic and in his own words so perfect that he was quasi-legally and certainly morally entitled to consider himself the real thing.'

At this point I couldn't restrain myself. 'And of course you keep these deluded clones, or one might say deluded drones, in secure and profitable employment, don't you, Des?'

That was a bad sign. I always call him Des when I am about to take umbrage or take aim.

Liz flinched and made all-purpose chin gestures at both of us indicating cool it, stop it, don't start it, don't bloody row at a time like this of all times. But Desmond had had a fair quantity of my costly 2001 reserve port, and it was emphatically not a tribute port but a real one, and he was not to be squashed by a senile bully such as me.

'Oh oh,' he snorted. 'I wondered when the lecture would start. I noticed you had been unreasonably friendly for at least twenty minutes.'

'Oh come on, man,' I replied. 'I'm not patronising you, I'm challenging you! Pretend we are two students hot in debate and determined to seek out the truth, instead of one old lag working in regional arts admin pitted against the old lag's geriatric Dad who is footling about in the hotel trade.'

'I think . . .' interposed Liz.

'I think,' I inter-interposed, 'that you are an indispen-sable and culpable part of the support system of these pathetic plagiarists, Des. If you pulled the plug out and refused to hire them the public would be starved of their idiotic addiction and . . .'

'Would stay at home swilling lager and watch a cute telly programme about other people's favourite and/or most bizarre sexual postures? Or about making lots of selfish dosh out of buying and selling charming old renovated London slums. Or about someone very posh and pampered, and the poor posh soul is forced to spend a week in the bedlam house of someone unutterably dog rough, unemployed and boorish. On the principle of let's put a dog and a cat together in a closed cage and enjoy the educative spectacle.'

'Exactly,' I said. 'Exactly. I'm glad you agree that modern entertainment culture is terminally debased to the point of terminally diseased. First principles agreed, that's good. But why do you, young Desmond, have to be as morally rank as good old Quentin and Letitia, the notional BBC 2 and Channel 4 programmes schedule chiefs in dear old, dirty old 2008?'

Desmond grinned as if he really were a twenty-year-old student who didn't give a damn about being called morally rank, it was all just words after all.

'Because Quentin and Letitia, if they are like me, probably have families. Families need money, they really do, Dad, it is the most basic stonewall fact to hit anyone between the eyes who is over the age of seventeen. The stone wall will not go away no matter how much you huff and puff and try to blow the bastard down. It can't be exploded by dynamite, it can't be willed away by hypnosis, it . . .'

'Yes it can,' I snorted.

'No it can't,' said Liz with moderate exasperation. 'You have survived your seventy-three years by fluke economics, Joe, but the whole world can't operate in that sunny manner. You had me to support you up until Harrison left you a fortune, and since then you've managed to lose most of it on account of your absolute principles.'

'Bah,' I said. 'It wasn't my fault the cookery books I

slaved over didn't sell. I didn't compromise myself by going away and writing a book called *Cooking With A View To Improving How You Fuck* or *Cooking For Extra Brain Power* or *Dockland Penthouse Cuisine Made Extra Easy For The Gormless Posh*.'

'Maybe you should have,' said Desmond. 'You tell me I am supporting something that is morally wrong, that I am an inextricable part of a compromised structure. But you can only please yourself because others support you. I didn't have your fairytale windfall. Nor did I have someone like my mother to support me for forty-odd years. You can only be so pure in your principles because someone else has made the impure lucre.'

I snorted, 'It is all relative. Money comes and goes like everything else, but sticking to first principles stops us being crude laissez-faire idiots. This business of bedfellows, Des, where would you draw the bloody line? What I want to know is how can you possibly live with yourself hiring mountebank fortune tellers by the cartload down there in poor old Wilts?'

He sighed as if engaged in dialectic with an importunate four-year-old.

'Clairvoyants, not fortune tellers! They are a sell out. I could put on one a week and they'd still be a sell out. It is what the public clamours for and I have no option but to give it them. As it is they subsidise the two string quartet performances that we put on every year.'

'Eh? Which string quartets? By whom?'

'What the hell's that got to do with it?'

'Think Josef Haydn would be pleased you're subsiding him with a stargazer called Gladys or a soothsayer called Doug? He'd sooner you didn't fucking perform him at all!'

'Don't be so absurd. Try being realistic for once in your life. How the hell would you know what financial compromises someone like Haydn had to make when he was alive? Got a direct line to him have you?'

'No, it is your Glad and your Doug who have the direct lines! And when these homespun occultists aren't captivating your willing Wiltshire dupes, you have the rent-a-grin copycat tributeers instead. Think Claude Debussy or Maurice Ravel would be delighted that Frank Byfield, Mitch Bygraves or the Kenny Bell Band are selflessly responsible for the Wiltshire burgers getting their biannual rations of French chamber music?'

At that point another kind of music erupted. Liz suddenly raised her hand to her mouth and gave a demented elephant's trumpeting sound. Father and son stopped in mid-shout and stared at her in consternation. She said:

'All this is driving me mad, so I'm going to give you both a paradoxical injunction! Joe Gladstone, try with every atom of your being to be as wilfully unkind and unsympathetic to your son as you can, and try above all to row hard enough to drive him away for the next ten years. Desmond, don't to the smallest degree restrain yourself, do rise to the bait at every opportunity, do give your father a strict tit for tat even when he seems to be all puerile rhetoric rather than reason . . .'

Desmond smiled and looked as if he was ready to respond obediently to her deliberately contrary and perverse advice. But I was not seduced by the impromptu Zen approach.

'Look,' I said threateningly, inordinately irritated by that smile of his. 'It is more than just art and bloody arts centres that are at stake. The world will manage without them in the long run. It will also manage without Desmond's psychic conjurors and starry-eyed conduits of the spirit world. But it has suddenly occurred to me, you know, as blinding revelation, that this tribute motif has far wider applications than mere derivative entertainment. Why, it seems to explain a hell of lot of things, up to and including power politics of the vaudeville UK variety. Mean to say, Des, wouldn't you agree that Mr Anthony Blair of happy memory was a successful tribute act to the Iron Lady of happy memory, when in her ferrous prime? What did he call himself, what was his sell-out tribute stage name, Des? Ah yes, The Iron Laddo. (Not to be confused with his identical twin brother The Virtuous Head Boy.) Almost put her out of business didn't he, why, they almost preferred his unbending iron to the original non-ductile variety?' I had been gurgling on stanchlessly, and by now Liz had her eyes raised skywards at my bugger-you-all eloquence. 'Yes,' I finished and not without a certain anticlimax, 'the tribute copycat method of political analysis seems a damn fine universal model to me. I wonder why no one else has thought about it before?'

I forgot to say I had been knocking back twice as much of the priceless reserve Offaly's as my son, a prelude as ever to a rhetorical flood or do I mean an imaginative swamp?

Liz said, 'Ah, very entertaining. On that model you, Joe, would be a tribute act to one of those monomaniac ranters in George Bernard Shaw plays. Crossed with someone like George Formby minus his ukulele but plus his trademark grin. The trouble with you is you can't allow other people to lead their own lives and you want Desmond here . . .'

Desmond couldn't resist the obvious checkmate: 'To be a tribute act to *you*, Dad. You would like nothing better in the whole world than for me to be a copy-cat but inevitably inferior version of yourself.'

Further and very brief instalment of *Galluses Galore*

(Scene, centre of Great Border City, erstwhile City Of The Nineties, spring 2018. All adult male citizens mournfully but obediently exposing their braces except for . . .)

Fenton Baggrow eventually became suicidally reckless in his disregard of the new pilot-scheme legislation, so fearless in his flagrant flouting that it was almost as if he wished to provoke the authorities into a brutal over-reaction (*a bessic if nut acnied Knee-o Trutskyisht manyeuver, even if Fenten issel wuss allus mare ev an oot an oot Noth Cummlan Hannykisst*). One cold February day he took to cycling through the middle of Carlisle – and it was bustling Continental Market day, to make it even worse and some of the visiting French and Belgian cheese sellers were uproariously entertained – draped from head to foot in a long black cloak of impressive billowing dimensions (*raither like an owd orrer moofy fillon, an ter cap aw Fenten ed this bliddy greet mask wid a daft farm yakker's fyass stuck on it. An guess wat else wuss pentit on t'lyeugs ev t'mask?*). On his facetious rustic yokel mask Fenton, who was not without a considerable innate pictorial talent, had also painted a colossal and threatening pair of galluses loops that had succeeded in pulling the yokel's lugholes completely flat against his skull. (*Teknikly in 2018 Fenten wuss byath leekel and illeekel. Hooiver, cos t'galluses wuss foorchal raither than rill, t'owd Carel pleece thowt that amoontit till bare-fyasst impidence raither than creatif élan er wassacomie yon udder Frensh wood 'oopry'.*)

Fenton was chased on foot by three policemen but he succeeded in vanishing down one of those narrow lanes behind the cathedral and tossing his cloak and mask into a handy recycling bin. As for his bicycle he stashed that inside the same recycling bin, pulled the cover to, and bolted it with his own hefty lock. He returned for it at dead of night when the area was deserted and cycled back at his leisure in the direction of the A689 (*an pantin like buggery he stoppt off at t' Witshiff Inn at Farlum an ed issel alf a dozen pints, an an extra pakit ev Whoosher Soss krishps fer luck*).

End of instalment of *Galluses Galore*

As for Elizabeth's romance it proceeded not by stealth and deviance but by ineluctable animal magnetism so she claimed . . .

For once I have called her by her proper Christian name, because it has a special poetry that her usual name does not have. Liz as a name suggests someone friendly, pert, humble, comic, approachable, resilient, adventurous, ambiguous and more. Remarkably every single one of those adjectives could apply to my wife, and I could never exhaust her nuances or her imaginative possibilities. Why should it be that that single syllable Liz should be so infinitely allusive and might signify or suggest almost anything? By contrast the four syllable Elizabeth has a specific and tender solidity about it, a definite suggestion of poetry and gravity. Again, all that applies to my wife, which is why, despite my frequent grumbling and sniping at her, I know that she is worth everything in the world, and I will never find another like her as her like does not grow on trees.

She kept being invited back to the monthly rock concerts by Marge the café owner and Jane who sold antiques. And of course Jane's brother Patrick, who was sixty-two but looked fifty, was always there like a pox or a village-hall air vent or a village-hall fire alarm or a village-hall tea urn. After the boogie-woogie of Reverend Wiley and the All Stars came a Balkan fusion band from Glasgow called Sofia's Boys. It was an allusion lost on some of the audience including boozy Marge, who didn't know the name of the Bulgarian capital, and vaguely thought it had something to do with a charismatic TV crime series called *The Sopranos*. They were geniuses at mixing jazz with Balkan gypsy music even if they were all native Glaswegians with very strong accents. Their leader, a clarinet player called Tam, did not tear up any Bibles for his finale, he did nothing more blameless than dance frantically on one leg whilst shouting out and trilling at his clarinet, arguably in homage to a recent movie by that other genius Emir

Kusturica, someone whom both Liz and I could watch until the Balkan cows come home.

Yes, she mentioned the films and music of Kusturica when she mentioned Sofia's Boys, and I winced at the tangential association. It caused me considerable jealous pain that one of our favourite film directors should be even remotely allied with the arrival of an insidious third party. Because Patrick Garnett, this time in a light white jacket and white chinos and designer white plimsolls, meaning that he was now a sixty-year-old passing for a fifty-year-old passing for a twenty-five-year-old . . . this one destined to vanish up his own designer-clad arse in terms of chrono-logical regression so that he might one day come out the other side as minus forty, minus sixty etc. etc. . . . Patrick loved the Balkan fusion music even more than the Bible-tearing boogie-woogie man. Garnett was as fit as a flea as well as being as rank as one in my view . . . and he danced all night without drawing breath. He hardly touched the paint-stripper plonk for one thing, and so remained talking sense for most of the night. He knew that Liz fancied him and true enough he fancied Liz but it was Jane who was driving tonight, and Liz could therefore drink and drink she did. She particularly admired Garnett's abstinence and a related feature which was that although he enjoyed dancing with Liz and hardly danced with anyone else, he enjoyed just as much dancing on his own.

'On his own,' I rapped suspiciously, although in retro-spect I was very pleased. This was I seem to recall night number two of the wretched week of Liz's confessional. 'Well that was a definite warning sign.'

'What do you mean?' she asked me with red, red eyes which were as puffy and wasted as shrunken tulips.

'A man who dances on his own? Bah. Either a gross unreformed narcissus or a sexagenarian hippy. You recall how male hippies used to close their eyes and shake their heads in a perpetual motion trance at rock festivals,

Woodstock and the like? And come to think of it those rural rock concerts often attract some very senile beautiful people who settled here in Cumbria in the early Seventies. They were born circa 1940 and these bouncing war babes are now gaga old peace babes, isn't that true?'

'Patrick is not and has never been a hippy. He's a lecturer in Newcastle with an enormous–'

'Stop there,' I snapped, and added the merciless saloon-bar innuendo line. 'I have no wish to know how well hung the dear boy was.'

'Stop it.' An enormous brain! He has a huge brain and could no more be a hippy than you or I could.'

'But you say that the man likes to dance with himself, which I would say is surely a variation on him playing with himself?'

'As it happens I was impressed, wrongly as it turns out, by his apparent independence. He was happy to dance with me and show interest in me, but equally he was happy to dance on his own, as if he was self-sufficient and his own man.'

I drummed my vindictive fingers. 'Self-sufficient rather than a self-abuser. Or maybe both on close forensic analysis, what?'

After about five of these rural rock performances, the magnetism definitely beyond all calibration by now, Liz and Patrick ended up back at his place . . . a beautiful seventeenth-century Debatable Lands farmhouse stuck up a half-mile stony track. Parnell had a 4 by 4, bless him, to cope with such strenuous inaccessibility and to get him to and from his demanding Newcastle lecturing job. Bear in mind that our doughty adulteress was seventy, and here was her toy-boy of sixty-two who was a virtual toy-boy of fifty. Using the Desmond Gladstone tribute model, an existential poetics derived from my son's artistic groundwork with his tribute bands, Patrick at sixty was a tribute to himself at fifty: he had become his own best and amazingly lifelike homage.

Looking back I ought to have rapidly enough seen what was going on. But after deviously comparing notes, as if the problem were a notional one rather than my own, with one or two drinking pals who had been cuckolded in public as it were, I have learnt that it is amazing what one can fail to see. In any event, Liz and he would bump their way up the rough old dirt road in Patrick's gas guzzler, dally until about two or three, whereupon he would run her back to The Lonning and leave her at a discreet distance down the road. I was usually fast asleep and regularly exhaling retsina fumes, a bit like a one-man pine forest or aromatic pine glade. The next morning she would tell me Marge or Jane had dropped her off and I would nod vaguely and tell her I was pleased she had enjoyed herself at something more radically youthful than chutney-bottling or embroidery. Little did I know. Occasionally their adulterous routine varied, and both of them would stay sober and drive in separate cars back to his place. She would leave her little saloon parked at the start of the track, and they would proceed the rest of the way in his armoured tank on the grounds that the dirt road would knacker her little car's sump or worse.

'Bugger your sump,' I said rather witlessly at this point in her confessional. In fact I was only repeating the tail end of her last sentence, but she thought I was swearing at her with an unusual car mechanic's epithet.

'I wish you weren't so aggressive,' she said crying and making raw little snottering noises. 'I know that I deserve it but–'

'Exactly,' I said. 'After this adventure of yours, you and I, Liz, are extreme not to say freakish statistical rarities. I would sooner not be quite so freakish. You have opted to have your first affair in your eighth decade and after forty-five years of marriage. If you'd done it when you were thirty after five years marriage, I would have had five years hurt and anger to swallow. After ten years, ten years etc. Instead I have a full forty-five years worth of wounded feelings and aching wretchedness to cope with, so a bit of ugly irony and vicious sarcasm are in order I think. I don't believe in violence but even if I did I can't knock you about to relieve my feelings because you are far stronger than I am and would twist my arm and hurl me to the floor.'

Liz smiled and obviously took my vaudeville image as some indication of wished-for light relief and therefore a nascent glimmer or forgiveness whence reconciliation. Bear in mind that in this same week of confession she had told me about the powerful literal vision she had had of a thing so gentle and unresistant that it cannot be destroyed . . . of something undeniably holy . . . and from a source which she for one reckoned to be the one and only source.

But I did not smile back at her. I was unamused by the cartoon image of her flinging me on the ground with those strong and very beautiful and infinitely familiar arms of hers.

'I'm not laughing,' I told her with a face of unrelenting granite. 'I'm really not laughing at anything at all.'

6

Exactly forty-eight hours after the copious Greek banquet
(much of it those deliriously succulent balls, balls, balls you
might recall), Pargeter, Dixon, Marjorie and Cora had the
following slung at them:

Menu of Gujerati-style Indian banquet served at
The Lonning, 8 p.m., 8 December 2008

stuffed small brinjals
(cumin seed and hing/asafoetida are fried in oil in a large
pan. Next small brinjals/aubergines/eggplants are cut into
four half way through, a masala of cumin powder, coriander
and garam masala rubbed into the exposed surfaces, and
the eggplants placed carefully in the same oil. Yoghurt
mixed with besan/gram flour is then poured over, and they
are covered and stewed on a very low heat. When almost
done green chillies, sugar and salt are stirred in, and the
little brinjals are reverently cooked as in a hypnotic dream
to aromatic perfection)

shakariya dabada
(sweet potatoes are peeled and cut into long slices. They
are stacked in pairs like quaint orange sandwiches, and are
filled with an elaborate and unhinging masala of coconut,
coriander leaf, ginger, chillies, roast gram, hing, lime juice,
salt and sugar. The orange sandwiches are fried in oil and
cooked oh so tenderly in a covered pan)

mitho-limbdo raita
(fried curry leaves, dry roasted cumin seeds and green
chillies are thoroughly pounded to an odoriferous paste.
This very pungent masala is stirred into a bowl of good
fresh yoghurt along with mustard seeds and hing which
have been fried in oil)

biraj pullao
(dry rice is fried in best butter with a teaspoonful of sweet
cardamom seeds, then cooked in a closed pan with the
requisite amount of water. When almost done channa dal
(Bengal gram) and sugar are added, the lid replaced and
cooking continued. The rice is turned out onto a handsome
ceramic bowl and a quantity of fried pistachios, cashews,
almonds and raisins is judiciously mixed in, plus a delicate
swish of saffron essence)

And so on. Among other things I also gave Pargeter and the
rest of them *khajur raita* (dates ground with coconut and
folded into yoghurt) and another deliriously sweet pullao
aromatised with rosewater and grated nutmeg. Finally,
and just to show I wasn't all sugary sweetness and light, I
threw at them with a grim health warning *mirchi nu shak*
which is a lunatic incendiary dish of long green chilis fried
with a masala of roasted coconut, poppy seeds, sesame
seeds, mustard seeds, cumin seeds, pounded peanuts . . .
lime juice, salt, sugar and yet more chilli for the suicidal to
savour.

I take it you fail as a rule to get this kind of thing in your
local tandoori or carry-out (ext. which is 1-ed 2)? Have you
ever wondered why it is that ninety-five per cent of our
'Indian' restaurants aren't run by Indians, but by Bangladeshis, and ninety-five per cent of those are from the same
circumscribed region of Sylhet? And yet these Sylhetis

105

obligingly knock out Dhansaks which are Bombay Parsee, as well as other dishes staunchly called Malaya, Madras, Kashmiri etc. They bravely take on the whole subcontinent and make a remarkably accomplished job of it, all considered. The reason I mention all this geographic stuff is a piquant one. Take it from me that what I make when I cook an Indian spread tastes very nice, mirchi conflagrations and last wills and testaments aside. But there is – how can I put it? – a significant, overarching and intractable problem.

It tastes very good, my Gujerati food, but it doesn't, despite the salivating clamour of fans like Bill Pargeter and Marjorie Staff . . . it doesn't, how shall I phrase this with due impartial candour and an absence of unseemly disingenuousness? . . . it's just that good as my Gujerati food tastes, *it doesn't really taste Gujerati*. Instead, and it pains me to say this, it tastes bloody *North Cumbrian Gujerati*!

There. I've said it. I don't have the right and authentic sort of ghee and the right authentic sort of jaggery, you see. I don't have the echt indigenous ingredients without which any foreign cuisine is always going to be a pale as opposed to powerful imitation. I am more like a Cumbrian tribute chef . . . to a real and original Gujerati chef, if you follow me. Even though someone like adamant Pargeter will generously insist that on the evidence of his senses I must be as good as the real thing.

The point is that, though he has been all over the globe on his Harley, Pargeter has never been to India, much less Gujerat. So how could he possibly know?

I still have a number of relatives, most of them very old, in the industrial west of this very large county. They live between forty and fifty miles away, meaning they are equidistant with bustling millennial quayside Newcastle, Baltic Gateshead etc. All of a sudden the latter has all the northern glamour and the cachet, while West Cumbria, God bless it, has absolutely none. In parts down west the dialect is so strong it really does sound like a forgotten foreign language. They use verbs that are purest unreformed Norse and in this digital age when supposedly we ought to be speaking the same identical argot, meaning a refined Basic English with only two real verbs that matter, namely 'to text' and 'to chill', they still use the words *lait, laik, kyav* and *skop* dozens of times a day.

Lait (Old Norse *leyta*) is used principally in the sense of to bring or fetch or carry, an interesting extension of its proper meaning to 'seek' or 'search out'. This supple and subtle dialect vocabulary extrapolates effortlessly across linguistic barriers into my own life. Earlier I said I had no idea whatever about my inscrutable wife carrying on with the lecturer Garnett, but the truth of the matter is I had an inchoate, nameless and persistent anxiety about something very worrying, though I knew not what. If I had pursued it to its instinctive end, followed my hunches and in doing so followed Liz, metaphorically and then literally to wherever she was heading, I would soon have made the feeling match the chilling truth of things. My husbandly anxiety would have had me watching her movements, her actions, her phone calls, her departures and returns in the car at unusual hours, though give her her due always with the most convincing excuses. I would then have *laited* Liz, meaning I would have pursued and sought her out (at those wild and motley rock concerts; in Garnett's remote and inaccessible farmhouse) and the same verb would also accommodate the deed of my bringing or fetching, even carrying her protectively, angrily, dementedly, tyrannically back home.

The verb *laik*, sometimes written *lake*, would also have had its part in the painful and complex scenario. It means to play (Old Norse *leika*) but its earliest signification was probably to jump about or to dance. Need I say more?

Liz and Garnett leapt about and danced to the music of Reverend Wiley or Sofia's Boys when they also played together like two cavorting lambs. In either event they *laiked* like buggery in good old rampant Nordic style. *Kyav*, also written *keav* (Old Norse *kafa*), could also have been employed expressively and allusively to depict the unfolding drama. It is used strictly in the sense of to kick these days, though its original meaning was the vigorous turning of hay or straw whence a secondary derivation of pawing restlessly as in the case of a horse. Liz was doing much of the latter, restless pawing in the obvious and lurid sense during the love affair, and restless fidgeting when the truth was coming to light with her horrified husband. No kicking as such took place but had I cornered them *in flagrante* in the dance hall or his farmhouse I would have kicked her home and him in all directions. And *skop* meaning to throw or fling, and with no other antecedent meaning as far as I know, would have described my infuriated motor movements as I threw her out of his arms and flung him in his lovely turquoise tailored jacket out of the fucking picture.

Further instalment of *Galluses Galore*

Fenton Baggrow not only went in for flamboyant direct action in a city centre, he also went in for sly revolutionary propaganda in the rural public houses. Just as in true street-theatre style he had cycled through Carlisle in a Vincent Price cloak and clownish mask to satirise the Compulsory Braces Act . . . so he now took every opportunity to expatiate (*spit fleein aw ways wid sek turrenshal elkwance!*) on the hypocrisy and double standards of the ones who framed these tyrannical and pointless laws.

These orations did not take place exclusively in Cumbria. Baggrow was regularly to be found speechifying uninhibitedly (*wid a gob like a greet torn pockit*) in some pub lying just inside the Northumbrian border and hence outside of the pilot-scheme area. Because of that tantalising braces-free zone aspect, it would usually be full of Cumbrians who had driven, walked or cycled across the border and now strutted around the bar and saloon as if they didn't have a care in the world. By an inverse logic not a few Northumbrians liked to sally in the opposite direction and have a drink in a nearby Cumbrian pub. Here they gladly twanged at their dusted-off antique braces which were obligatory temporary dress for anyone visiting Cumbria: Dutch and Japanese tourists included. Sad to say, all of these foreigners, Northumbrians and men from the Dumfriesshire and Roxburghshire Scots side, loved this ritualised vicarious braces-wearing in the same way that small children enjoy dressing up for the harmless fun of it. Or alternatively in the same way that people enjoy visiting Madame Tussaud's to see how the waxworks are thriving and to congratulate themselves they are not permanently frozen and imprisoned museum pieces like these (*cos they can allus pish off oot ev Cummerlan juss when it syeuts, an skop their bliddy galluses reet ter t' back ev t'Nothumlan er t'Dutsh waardrub*).

'Can you mind,' announced Baggrow, one February night in a badly lit Northumbrian bar which was heaving with Cumbrians all blithely sporting belts the width of skirting boards, 'can you mind, all you folk, back to 1982?'

To which there was a considerable blank response as the fifty-odd drinkers scratched their chins in the hopeless effort of recollection (*Fenten meant a guid thutty six 'ear sen, an maist ev them cudn't mind yesterday niffer mine ower a thud ev a bliddy sentry*).

'No we bloody can't,' they all eventually responded as a man.

The earnest quizmaster went on to stress that that year represented something momentous in the history of their country, a phenomenon unprecedented in the twentieth century, the nearest parallel being what had happened much earlier in 1939. Heavy and broad a hint as that was, not one of the *trans-flumen* (*t'hoppysit ev* kiss-floomen) Cumbrians nor any of the local Northumbrians knew what the eccentric orator was on about (*even if yah brainy feller Sissal Shimmins frae Lumley ed a CSE Grade Fower in Mutton Histry frae Halty High Schyeul in 1965*).

In the end Baggrow gave up the interrogation and pointed out that it was 1982 when Britain had dramatically waged unilateral war against a foreign country! This of course was not a precise parallel with Mr Chamberlain's declaration of 1939, when many other European countries had already been in conflict with the German foe . . . though the point such as it was seemed to float in the air rather than settle decisively on the heads of the struggling audience.

'Oh,' rose a puzzled clamour or just possibly a ripple from his dozy listeners. Those under the age of fifty, meaning no older than their mid-teens in 1982, shouted out as in a bona fide pub quiz, 'It was against Iraq!' (*Agyanst Hirak!*) or 'Against Afghanistan! (*Agyanst Afganistyan!*). Meanwhile many a slowcoach over fifty, possibly because their huge belts were so tight that their brains were temporarily parched of oxygen, also shouted 'Iraq!' and 'Afghanistan!', and a few tried Kuwait and Vietnam (*Kwet, Fetnam!*) for good measure. Only one of the assembly, a Northumbrian rather than a Cumbrian septuagenarian, put up his hand with the confidence of one who knows the correct answer.

'The Falklands, Fenton (*t'Fulklands, Fenten*)!' the Northumbrian cried.

More than one of the gathering thought he was objurgating an oath at Baggrow, but it was only the distortion of his Haltwhistle accent. Baggrow congratulated him warmly on his general knowledge and pressed the blushing old man to tell the crowd who it was the war had been waged against. The old man looked puzzled at that and said, *well we went an wished waar on t'Fulklands, Fenten as far as ah can mine.* At which Baggrow shook his head in dire exasperation and roared at the fifty-strong crowd that war was waged *on behalf of,* not against, the Falklands! Some of the younger lads claimed never to have heard of the Falklands which sounded to them like the name of a Cumbrian farmstead near Spadeadam or Bewcastle. They therefore found the whole riddle incomprehensible. Informed by an eighty-five-year-old Cumbrian from Midgeholme (*kwint owd Mitchum*) with a leather belt as big as a mantelpiece . . . that it was Argentina that Britain had waged war against apropos the Falklands, the non-comprehension was total.

The puce-faced prophet suddenly let loose mercilessly at his audience. He told them that, aside from the Midgeholme brainbox, they reminded him of the numerous local nincompoops who had been celebrating war against 'The Argies' (*t' Adgie Gadgies*) back in 1982! He, Baggrow, could vividly recall the thronging mob wandering round Carlisle when the war was announced, the boozed-up vaunting youths waving their fists against the Argie foe as if it were a competitive football team they were about to thrash as opposed to, in reality, attempt to decimate. Amazed at the sight of a warlike Cumbrian rabble in full throttle, Baggrow had on a sudden inspiration darted into Smith's newsagents and on the spot purchased a cheap World Atlas. Then recklessly walking into the middle of the roaring crowd he had slyly asked the ugliest of the assembly, a shaven-headed youth of twenty from Wigton called Kev, if he would kindly tell him where these wicked Argentinians lived, as he Baggrow hadn't a clue.

'Ah weel . . .' began Kev, pugnacious, defensive, drunkenly blinking in the blinding sunlight.

It was not just Wigton Kev who couldn't help the novice geographer. He looked at the map of Australasia upside down and hazarded that it was what was in fact New

Zealand stood on its head. Baggrow swiftly pointed out as much by way of shaming the Wigton warmonger, but Kev's friends Dez from Blencogo (*Cowga*) and Sid from Abbeytown (*Abba*) double-capped him by saying that the Aussies and Kiwis lived upside down anyway, everyone knew that. In any case who gave a fuck where bloody Argentina was, as long as it kept its evil hands off our priceless possession, the Falklands!

'Don't you see?' Baggrow implored his 2018 listeners enraged. 'Those buggers back in 1982 wanted the Argentinians' blood, even if they didn't know where Argentina was (*neah noshun where in t'bliddy hatless t'owd Adgie Gadgies lifft*)! They had never once given the place a passing thought till then. So then I asked them to show me the Falklands, and they pointed to Outer Mongolia (*Hooter Mangaly*), Surinam (*Surrey Numb*) and in one case a five-foot skinhead from Gretna put his thumb down on Sidcup (*Sid's bliddy Cap!*). And while this geography lesson was proceeding, would you believe it, in the telly shop opposite . . . guess who was on about twenty-five screens (*guid owd Madgie Thunder!*) and she was busy telling every Kev, Dez and Sid all over the country, that we the British were the greatest nation in the world (*best iffer widoot a doot!*). She also boasted we had the greatest army in the world (*widoot a bliddy doot!*). She also promised that we would win over all adversaries (*ivvry bliddy yan!*) . . . and that she had all of our loyal and precious country behind her, and . . .'

Then the absolutely incredible happened, and not even canny old Baggrow could have predicted such a thing. His audience, including those who hadn't even been alive at the time, all in retrospect stood loyal and reverent behind those timeless patriotic words of the immovable matriarch. One man in his sixties, a Northumbrian from Plenmeller called Stan, even began to warble the National Anthem with huge Northumbrian tears in his eyes. Then, and this took

Baggrow so much by surprise that he actually felt his blood sugar drop, and he realised it was ages since he'd had his last Mars Bar . . . then Fenton noticed something altogether sinister happening amongst the mass of his listeners. At first one, then two, then about six, then about twenty, then the whole bloody lot of them began fiddling uneasily around their waists. It was as if they were dusting off or shaking off some kind of noisome pollutants or invisible but direly noxious microbes. They were pawing restlessly, not unlike the movements of fidgeting horses at their uncomfortable midriffs (*they wuss kyavvin like hossis er dunkies in t'orishnal hettymelogical sense*).

Yes, but what exactly were they doing? Alas, it was all too shamefully obvious. They were one by one removing their belts! Not just the Cumbrians, who were on a busman's holiday from their galluses . . . but even the Northumbrians who could please themselves what they wore for the time being. They were all clumsily removing their belts, and they were all pawing restlessly and fidgetingly (*kyavvin, kyavvin, kyavvin like seah many restless owd cat hossis*) for the comfort and the virtue of their good old-fashioned braces.

N.B. (*Naughty Benny*)! Special addendum (*Speshul sek an sek stuck on t'tyal ev t'tyal*). You might be thinking that the masked cycle ride through central Carlisle and/or this vain attempt of Baggrow's at PPP (*pollytickle popgander in t'pups*) relate to his awesome whispered secret that shocked old Jakie Tunstall to the core. Recall that in a previous pub Baggrow had muttered some terrifying and complicated strategy he was planning against this idiotic government tyranny, and that this had caused old Tunstall grave alarm (*owd Jakie vanya shit a lintel er a him end niffer mind a bliddy brick*).

Well you're wrong (*thoo's awtergidder wrang*)! And they aren't. And the incredible hush-hush secret strategy is a great deal more disturbing than either of the above. And this being a 'Cummerlan Tyal' (*wid sundry oppligtry Red Erins, sister*) you'll have to wait a while to see what it is (*tho'll nid ter tyan tight hod ev thi rampant bliddy hossis*).

Meanwhile how exactly or even approximately did love develop in the extramarital case of my wife, the interior designer and venerable grandmother? If by some miracle of archive ferreting I were able to rifle back through the last forty years of the *Guardian* which I read from cover to cover six days a week, I have no doubt I would find an authoritative article about the age range for women embarking on their first, second, third etc. adulterous affair. But even by 2008 there must be a very low percentage starts the ball rolling at seventy, so all I can add is that someone has to be the one to break the mould, so why not my always original wife? And despite universal lip service to equal opportunities and combating prejudice against the old, a majority of people are severely unaware of a very elementary fact. Believe it or not, a seventy-year-old is at heart and by instinct absolutely no different at all to a forty-year-old or a twenty-year-old. I for one like footloose unpackaged foreign travel, all-night card games, original birthday presents, original Christmas presents, wild electric jazz and serenely harmonious classical music, and for that matter lots of pungent physicality with Liz, in the same way that I did in 1965 when I was thirty, in 1985 when I was fifty and in 1995 when I was sixty. Just because I look more or less like a donkey's backside aged seventy-three in 2008 doesn't mean I have the imagination and inner poetry of a donkey's arse. Or at least I don't think that to be the case . . .

As best I can I have to understand the maturation of Liz's feelings by her anguished account of it in that confessional week, in combination with my subsequent interrogation about the finer points, the precise chronology, the where this happened, the where that happened. That in itself is an interesting if painful point of reflection. Critical thinkers, scholars and academics are duly sceptical of what they call secondary sources, meaning a literary or impressionistic bird's-eye view or rapid survey of a certain area of knowledge. They prefer primary sources: original texts, original documents, contemporary accounts if we are talking history, or let us say biography with a dash of history in the case of Liz and Garnett. A study of first-hand sources usually implies being able to read them in the original language, which of course is not always English, and which is where the good old Brits rapidly come unstuck as most of them would sooner consume their own dung than consent to read and understand a foreign language.

Earlier I rendered the poetics of Liz's love affair in the absolute indigenous terms of the dialect, using the Nordic verbs *lait, laik, kyav* and *skop* . . . a wan flight of fancy and a joke perhaps, as neither Liz nor Garnett is exactly rooted and embedded in the landscape nor does either of them talk or think in the dialect. By contrast I was raised on a remote North Cumbrian hill farm and up until the age of about twelve in 1947 I spoke dense dialect as naturally as I did English. Ever since then I have been a bilingual who even if he wanted to cannot separate the two linguistic worlds as decisively and meaningfully as he ought. Even in conversation with metropolitan folk in 2008 I still find myself saying dialect 'wid' instead of 'with', a childlike regression to a simple dental rather than an effortful aspirate. This is not an affectation or a piece of chauvinistic whimsy, it is my natural linguistic reversion and template.

At the risk of boring you, I need to point out that when I say *wid*, whether I like it or not, I have a different signification and a wholly different semantic nuance than when I say 'with'. There is a different sense of modesty, comedy, and of personal insignificance with the former. I am in a different world with different eyes, a different snout and a different tongue. And when we move beyond a meagre preposition to the real world of discursive speech or thought, the principal inflection will always inevitably be comic as those Nordic vowels and diphthongs are all about long and drawn-out humorous distortion.

The sense of the comic is not to be confused with the facetious, just as my jesting sardonically about unfaithful Liz does not signify that I find it even remotely funny. The truly comic conforms to the dimensions of the soul, meaning it is deep and is always in a reversible equilibrium with the tragic or the sorrowful. I am currently in unashamed didactic mode, so let me tell you that my hero Charles Dickens is one of those rarities, the truly comic, because Charles Dickens among other things plumbs the depths of the grotesque, the cruel, the deformed, the desolate, the desperate and the lunatic, the fearful crenellations of the immeasurable because infinite soul. Whereas e.g. Messrs. Clive James, Ben Elton not to speak of ten thousand apprentice 'new' or 'alternative' comedians, no matter how hard they sweat, will never be truly comic, meaning truly funny, because they are far too infatuated with the merely associative one-liner. The one-liner alas will never be anything but an indication of shallow breath and ideation, something that comes and goes like froth on the sea or like a monotonous hiccup. The truly comic is all about deep breath, expansiveness, hugeness, a straining and intimation towards that which is limitless (q.v. Dickens, Rabelais, Flann O'Brien, and unfortunately not many more).

I am not indulging all this opinionated preamble for fun. There is method in my madness. This preliminary excursus on the dimensions of the soul as an explanation of the comic, is where we come to Liz and Garnett. At rock concert number four in the same village hall that saw the birth of their enamourment, Liz Gladstone had a second vision. Two visions within six months, that is, granted to a woman who had never had any at all in the previous seven decades!

Unfortunately for her the message of the first vision became conflated with the message of the second one in a way that apparently misled and confused her. In turn this made the parting with Garnett when it came, not only inevitable but far more painful than it might have been. It happened like this. They were dancing on the austere wooden boards of the village hall to a virtuoso jazz rock fusion band on tour from somewhere in the North East, possibly Darlington. The band were playing their own flawless versions of Weather Report standards as well as tributes to Stanley Clarke, Al Di Meola and Jean-Luc Ponty. In this case the tributes were worked upon in brilliant improvisatory mode so be assured this wasn't one of my son's idiotic tribute bands, for the band did not pretend to be anything other than themselves. At one point a very slow and delicate number penned by the Austrian pianist Joe Zawinul, erstwhile colleague of Miles Davis, was performed, one of his inimitable signature tunes. Even in long lost North East Cumbria the tune was familiar and there was delighted clapping when it struck up. Liz and Patrick danced reverently to the beautiful, resonant even child-like pastoral tune, a hymn to childhood, landscape and a forgotten tender world.

About five minutes into the number Liz looked at Garnett under the red dance hall lights and saw him utterly transformed . . .

This is where it gets difficult to be precise because unfortunately I am your secondary source, I am not Elizabeth Gladstone, the only one who saw what she saw. And as she herself found it difficult to put it into words, with the best will in the world I am bound to let my own jealous perspective colour things. At any rate it was Garnett's beautiful eyes that were the source of the mystery. They were deep blue, a gentle blue, and as Liz glanced tenderly at those eyes of his she felt the steady and relentless shifting of registers, of the usual safe perceptual coordinates.

Once again Garnett though dancing with her was also dancing for himself and on his own. And in contrast to my wounded account of him as an exhibitionist, narcissus and onanist, he had instead this vivid appearance of someone uniquely and movingly as serene as a small child. He wore the precise innocence, according to my wife, of a young child. He had that same specific gentleness. He looked out-standingly as if like a child he would never hurt or harm anyone, if only because under this red dance-hall radiance he had attained a remarkable state of independence which was a function of his own mysteriously assured protection. It was as if Garnett would always be entirely and invisibly cared for, ineffably consummate and complete in his own right.

Faced with this inexplicable vision of Garnett's other-ness, Liz was both moved to the core and guiltily dismayed. He needed no one because he looked as if under a unique spiritual protection. As he moved his hands in simple rhythmic motions to the beautiful jazz which was all about childhood, tenderness and delicacy of memory, he was entirely sufficient to and for himself. He or his soul or what-ever was visible now underneath that transfixing light was indestructible and impossible to injure. And this of course was where she was reminded of her first vision where the torn up shreds of scripture flung on the ground by the boogie-woogie singer Rev. Wiley were the equivalent of this child's gaze before her. Because, all too clearly, neither the eternal Logos nor the spirit of a child could be translated by any conceivable means into non-existence . . .

But were these my wife's two visions of equal signifi-cance? Was this second vision, which was after all focused on a frail human rather than on sacred writ, a rather thin hallucination? Liz knew that when they stood outside the dance hall tonight, Patrick Garnett would not look much if anything like this vision of childlike innocence. He would have had a good deal of wine inside him apart from anything else, as she had opted to do the driving and to drink lemonade all night. Children didn't as a rule drink wine, nor more to the point did they have adulterous affairs. So all it might mean was that this vision of Patrick she'd glimpsed was only of one of his kaleidoscopic subtle facets, one of his 'selves', rather than the fullness of his soul. And this was where the spirituality as such was no longer of a classical scriptural sort. As such it was a vision that, painfully moving as it was, confused rather than clarified the truth of things.

7

The day after the mad shouting match with Desmond I went to visit my sister Sall, and Desmond to my irritation said he wanted to come along as well. I murmured of course, of course, why not, why not, and hoped he would pick up my soundless demur. Fat chance. But I could hardly try and talk him out of it, given they had been reasonably close aunt and nephew when she was in her right mind. I had this definite hunch that my driven and successful son would struggle with the floridity and hieroglyph communication at which Sall and her colleagues in Cherry Blossom House just outside Carlisle were such absolute experts. After all, the opposite of being driven and directed is being unfocused, divergent, random and repetitive, and my big sister Sall was all of that and a damn sight more.

My big sister Sall is rather small these days, in fact has shrunk to the size of a frail little shrimp. That said she has a colossal and powerful will, and will fight with the care assistants, the doctor, the hairdresser and anyone else who tries to get her to stand up when she wants to sit down, open her mouth when she wants it closed, close her mouth when she wants it opened, put her in a wheelchair when she prefers to lounge on the ground and eat from a kind of low slung card table. The table has been put there specially for her and spread beneath it is a cheerfully patterned vinyl cloth to catch the copious spillage. She rarely eats any of her meals in the central dining room, but in the thoroughfare adjacent, next to the reception, and a foot from the ground on the table which no one else is allowed to touch. In fact she spends nearly all of her waking hours close to the entrance and she does this because that is where all the action is, visitors and residents and staff alike will either navigate past or trip over her, she can see everybody coming and going, and can make a friendly or acerbic and demoralising commentary as it suits her.

'What a funny-looking bugger *he* is,' she will chortlingly exclaim at any passing woman who happens to have short hair. Then for good measure through her mirth: 'Sorry, son, but I think you look really stupid. I just can't stop laughing at the sight!'

Sall is seventy-six and lost her marbles at my age when she was seventy-three. I casually remarked as much to Desmond in the car and he looked at me presciently, possibly diagnostically. Last night I had more or less called him a compromised pimp in terms of his attitude to the provision of the arts in small town Wilts, and conceivably it had rankled. Perhaps such ugly choler and unbridled hectoring, he might be thinking, were signs of encroaching brain deterioration in his obstinate and impractical father. Given that pop in his loss-making guest house also consumed Kourtaki retsina as if there were no *avrio* or even any *methavrio*, the overall picture might be one of toxic albeit pine-resinated fumes relayed from the liver to the brainbox and there allowed perniciously to fester.

Sall was sat down on the floor next to reception and was dining from her special table. She was sipping coffee and eating some excellent-looking trifle and had long since discarded the spoon to get efficiently at the latter. She was scooping up the trifle in her grimy mitts and shovelling it in, cream, petrified custard and chromatic hundreds and thousands, oddly reminiscent of goldfish ant's eggs, mostly into her mouth but there were also a few bits going in her hair, on her nose and also dropping industriously down onto the floor. When she spotted any of the droppings, without hesitation she lunged at them with her fingers and swallowed the breathtaking mess with exemplary relish.

'Hallo, Sall,' I said, bending down to kiss a small portion of the back of her head after double checking it wasn't covered in grime-flecked cream or custard. Then straightening up again. 'What a pig's arse you're making of that trifle, you reckless bugger. What the hell are you doing playing tennis with it?'

'Joe?' she said, peering at me myopically as she won't wear her glasses and has given up reading and even watching telly. I do my best to visit her once a week and every time I see her I am startled by how she has seemingly aged in that modest interval. Then after about ten minutes the shock or more accurately the embarrassment of the sight will fade and the urge to entertain her will take its proper precedence.

'No,' I said. 'It's not me. It's Roy Rogers. Want to play Cowboys and Indians, Sall?'

I cackled energetically and kept up the teasing and before too long she was cackling back, more or less convinced it was me, her daft kid brother.

Desmond flinched at my rumbustious address as he no doubt expected me to talk to her in hushed tones and with forensic tweezers, the way a great many folk talk to the odd, the forlorn and the senile. But I always talk teasingly to Sall the confused, just as I did when she was Sall the non-confused, a mere three years ago. My logic is that if doughty Sall of 2005 could see me talking to Sall the shrunken but resilient shell of 2008, she would wish me to treat her as her old self, not as some tragic and pitiful case. But Desmond, unable to visit her with my frequency, thought I was being all too bluff rather than kind. He stooped down and tenderly kissed her on her creamy, dirt-covered lips, a brave and moving gesture I thought, until I saw him reach for his hanky and keep on wiping worriedly at his mouth for the rest of our visit.

'What's new?' I asked her. 'Anything fresh, Sall?'

She ignored me and stared critically at this middle-aged man who had kissed her. 'Who the hell's that?'

'Eh? It's Desmond.'

'Who?' she said incredulous, as if I had said Bob Hope or Lenny the Lion.

'My pardner the Cisco Kid. Bah, you know damn fine who Desmond is. He's my son. He's your nephew. Stop buggering about. Of course you recognise him.'

'No I bloody don't! Hang on. Look. Over by the door. That's not Sam, is it?'

Sam was a small boy she had known in the tiny rural school back in 1938 when she was six. He had been killed in a farm accident and she now went through for the umpteenth time the hellish aftermath of the seventy-year-old tragedy. Sam's younger sister Mary had been brought round to sleep in Sall's bed the night of the accident, in the hope that the company of an older girl would soothe her. But she had cried inconsolably and been taken back to the bereaved parents whose only remaining child she was. I explained this briefly *sotto voce* to Desmond who didn't know the story, and I could see him asking himself why he made so little an impression on Sall that she preferred to look at long-dead phantoms a couple of yards behind his head.

Luckily, there was a distraction. Connie, who is eighty, fine-boned, handsome and favours immaculate and expensive pastel suits, came sauntering through from the dining room. She has an expansive and charming smile but her communication is peculiarly rigid, as if she is parroting some bizarre and curmudgeonly parental lore of seventy-odd years ago. I offered her one of Sall's sweets, and after a reluctant refusal she started a shrill and dogged monologue about struggling against eating the whole packet, and no, even that wouldn't be enough, she'd be so greedy she'd naughtily want to eat a whole sweet shop, and no beyond that a whole sweet factory, and then beyond that . . .

'Shakespeare was probably the same as you,' I said judicially. 'Victor Hugo ditto. Huge men, huge artists, huge appetites. Here, have a sweet Connie, have the whole bloody packet and it'll do you a world of good. You know you need to stop all this denying yourself nonsense. What was it Hugo once said? "All I need to keep me going is soup and whores!" Can you remember, Desmond? Or was that Godfrey Wynn said that?'

Desmond flushed and chided my shameless quotation. I was just about to point out that at eighty and with her beautiful looks Connie might know rather more about the facts of life than either of us, when she herself bridged the impasse. She pointed admiringly at surly-looking Sall.

'Whereas this little lady here, this little girl Sall, she will just eat and eat and eat for evermore!'

She could have improvised for the next hour like an opera coloratura about ingestion and non-ingestion, greed and abstinence, satiety and indulgence, and about her limitless understanding of all related phenomena. Luckily Tom, a recent arrival of about seventy-five, who has been her boyfriend since day one, came sidling up behind her. Smiling tolerantly at Desmond and me, he put his arm round Connie's waist and in a pleasing baritone began to sing an old-fashioned song with great passion and conviction. He had a fine, sensitive, expressive face, and a large nose which ought to have spoiled his looks but somehow improved them. Nevertheless dressed in a fashionless old man's green cardigan, he was a let-down sartorially speaking beside Connie in her sumptuous two-hundred-pounds green suit.

Tom led Connie off by the waist into the dining room and she raised her blue eyes at his importunate ways.

'This man,' she declared, 'will *not* leave me alone!'

I said, 'Good. Congratulations. The best problem you could have in my view. Don't hold back like you do with the Maltesers. It doesn't matter if you go through a whole army of men like a dose of salts . . . they can't shoot you for it at our age. And what a grand voice your chap has, Connie. A bit like Jim Reeves crossed with Mario Lanza.'

Desmond cleared his throat uneasily then stiffened as Sall commented maliciously at Connie's departing back: 'Last week . . .'

She stopped dead, as if preparing us for something serious. I sat up all ears as it were at such temporal specificity. Sall's usual habit these days was to conflate seven seconds ago with seventy years ago, so to hear her talking about last week was something of a profound narrative shift.

'Yes?' I prompted her. 'Last week what?'

She looked irritated as if my repetition was refutation rather than encouragement.

'Of course it was last week!'

'OK,' I snorted. 'OK, clever clogs. I'm not disputing it. But either tell us all about last bloody week or shut up and whack out the Maltesers.'

'Last week she *shit* on that wall behind you!'

Desmond gulped and moved away from the wall. I myself did not gulp but said, 'Who?'

'Her!'

'You mean Connie?'

'Of course! And the week before that she pissed on the wall.'

'Aha,' I said. 'Are you sure of that? If so, I wonder to what purpose.'

'Because she's man-mad. She'll go with anything!'

A magnet for the males even though she urinated and defecated on institutional walls on a weekly basis? I chuckled at Sall's wild fib, and then out of nowhere felt suddenly and painfully emotional. I felt above all how completely impossible it would be to explain to my mad sister that my wife, her sister-in-law, had had an affair at the mad age of seventy and that as a result I was as wounded as a stricken beast. Even stranger I half wanted to tell Desmond about his mother's perverse behaviour, not to punish or betray her, but to let him know that for all he was middle-aged, educated, salaried, secure, he knew bugger all about life really. In the real world which was often as mad as Bedlam, life was not a business of mimetic tribute music but of real music however discordant by real originals. Connie for example might well be trussed up by ancient and constricting parental injunctions, but at eighty she still could effortlessly pull the blokes in an arena where the dance room coordinates were rather different from the ones where Liz and Patrick had found each other. After all a residential care home is not exactly a relaxed arbour of love or a romantic playground, but fastidious Connie and Tom the crooner had managed to make it so to an impressive extent.

Or had they? Ten minutes later Tom came past us and his crooning had stopped. In his bottle-green cardigan he explained worriedly to father and son that he had to get back to Carlisle urgently to see to his shop. There was a new lad starting with paper deliveries and he needed to show him the ropes. He then headed in haste for the front door which was of course security coded, stared at it uncomprehending, turned on his axis and then returned to us.

'Roadworks,' he snorted. 'There's roadworks and you can't get past the bastards for love or money.'

'Oh?' I said. 'So who'll see to your shop? And whereabouts did you say it was?'

He named an old-fashioned newsagent's which I knew to have closed down about a decade ago. Acute, painful to behold anxiety entered his eyes as he battled to think of how he could get past the roadworks to help the dozy delivery kid who in reality must be of marriageable age by now. Suddenly it providentially occurred to me that if this had been Desmond aged five fretting about the impossible,

I would have practised the age old remedy of . . . distraction.

'Not to worry,' I said. 'If I were you I'd go and see to your girlfriend over there. I might be wrong but I think she has something on her mind and she needs your protective arms around her. She's definitely the best-looking woman in the place but she's looking bloody restless, know what I mean? Meanwhile, listen, after we've gone, me and my son will pop round to check everything's OK at your papershop. Don't worry, I know exactly where it is. As it happens, I run a little business myself, and I know all about organising staff.'

At that point I could have sworn I heard Desmond say, 'Like fuck!' Aside from the fact he is not given to cursing and certainly not in front of old ladies, I couldn't work out whether he was scoffing at The Lonning's non-existent auxiliary staff, or spurning the perverse idea of encouraging this old man in his sad fantasy.

On the way home in the car he challenged me on precisely that:

'I'm not particularly convinced you're helping any of them by going along with their delusions. Apart from lying to that old Romeo about his shop, you told Aunty Sall you could see all the things she was seeing as plain as a pikestaff. Your mother and father who died in 1990, your grandparents who died in 1968, Uncle Harrison with his outsize leeks and his Senior bloody Maidens at the Newcastleton hound trails . . . even that poor little kid who died in an accident in 1938, you said you could see him too, and went on to outdo Sall about exactly how he looked.'

'Because it was the fifth time she'd told us about him! Once I started seeing him as well she shut up about it!'

And I pointed out the obvious: that I did it in the same simple spirit that I had gone along with Desmond's Cowboys and Indians or imaginary knights in armour when he was a small child. Had I tersely assured him aged six in 1966 that it was nonsense to believe in these incorporeal warriors, not only he but the whole adult world would have thought I was a repugnant monster for upsetting a child.

I went on, 'Sall's seventy-year-old memories really are all she has got, there is bugger all else in that sad little head of hers. I could I suppose ignore her memories and chat on informatively about suburban Carlisle 2008, which unfortunately means absolutely nothing to her by now. Or I could take a stern brotherly line, roll up my sleeves, tick her off, and demolish her nonsensical hallucinations one by one.'

'But encouraging someone's delusions can't possibly be doing them a kindness.'

'Who says?' I snorted. 'You have a lot to learn, my son. I told lover-boy Tom we were going to check his paper-shop was OK, because I guessed that it would ease his mind. So now, right enough, he's relieved and can concentrate on the rich poetry in his life, namely beautiful Connie. That's surely no different from me telling you when you were five, with suitable flourish and visual aids, that I had just sent the bogeyman packing out of your bedroom wardrobe. I even played the part of the fucking bogeyman squeaking, "Oh, I can't take being shouted at by your filthy-tempered old Dad, ooh ooh, off I bugger back to Bogeyland!" As for Lothario Tom, he may be seventy-five and incarcerated for his own safety, but he has his substantial joys. As well as hogging clothes-obsessed Connie he has a baritone that could stop a crowded city. That care home, which is by the way excellent, second to none in my view, Tom of course does not recognise it as such. He thinks he's in a short-stay hotel. I suspect it actually reminds him of some real overnight airport hotel he once stayed at. The non-existent roadworks that stopped him getting to his shop, the way he described them, there was a kind of stranded-on-the-M6-or-M74-on-your-way-back-from-Corfu flavour to it? The implication of that being that even his senile hallucinations have a real substratum, or to put it another way, his madness isn't completely mad.'

Desmond snorted and made some sarcasm about anti-psychiatry and R D Laing, a sad affiliation on my part to a now discredited 1960s charlatanry. At that I ought to have buttoned my lip but alas I couldn't restrain myself from giving him it unedited, uncensored and uncharitably.

'Each to one's own, eh boy? Your whopping income, your kids' skiing trips, your capacious semi in rural Wilts, they all come from exploiting the hallucinations of people who would claim to be sane rather than prematurely senile. Isn't it a fact that you let these deluded souls think they're watching the Beatles when they're actually watching the Battles or the Bottles or the Bushels? Or you let Sadie the stargazer with the funny eyes and the deep, deep voice, tell them they are going to have a lucky day next Tuesday, and especially if they are near running water (ooh and I *did* have a good Tuesday, and that day the tap really was spurting when I was brushing my teeth!). No one goes and puts *your* deluded punters in any remedial institution, nor indeed are you likely to be incarcerated for profitably deluding them. Meanwhile I charge Sall and Tom and Connie sweet f.a. for going along with their demented fantasies, whereas you charge fifteen quid a head for your kind of charlatanry. Then you no doubt smarm and smirk like a performing bloody poodle, and tell your fat-arsed PR-speaking West Country Regional Arts supremos that you are "strategically fostering" the arts in a "pragmatic mix and match" way and . . .'

Desmond did something rather startling at that point. He acted like a peremptory driving instructor and pulled the handbrake on until it squealed. Luckily we were dawdling the last mile or so on the deserted country road up to The Lonning and it was here he expressed the wish to get out and walk the fucking rest.

'And I'm cutting my stay short,' he shouted as he stomped away. 'I'm going up to Edinburgh tonight, not tomorrow.'
Oh God, I thought, and panicked. 'But your mother won't–'
'That's your problem!'
'Oh, she's my problem alright, Des.'
He stopped in his stride and stared at me. 'You what?'
'Nothing. Whatever you thought you heard, you misheard. Liz and I get on like a house on fire. Always have and always will. And don't go, Desmond, stay the night with us.'
But he didn't.

His mother turned on me in a rage once he'd driven off, having urged her to seek any explanation from her sheepish husband. She gazed at me incredulous as I told her that it was all to do with the way one deals with the deluded and the insane. I said all I'd done was go along with Sall's visions of the dead and Tom's obsessions with a non-existent shop, and that Desmond had taken fussy exception to my existential approach. Whereupon, and perhaps I'd overdone it, I'd pointed out how Desmond's meteoric career was all about profitably exploiting other people's 'sane' delusions.
'Great,' she said. 'So you drive away your one and only child on a ferocious point of principle. I hope you're bloody pleased.'
'It's more than that,' I said wearily. 'I know he's my son and I wish it were otherwise, but as a man he rather depresses me. He is old before his time, and he stifles me. I feel as if I am his wayward son and he is my stodgy old dad and I can't resist confronting him at times. Today he insisted on visiting his demented aunt assuming it might be a reasonably demanding but certainly not a harrowing outing. Senility unfortunately means brain deterioration,

cellular atrophy, linguistic and motor skills all in hellish disarray. The only way to make any headway with these poor old buggers is to enter their world as imaginatively as one can. Instead, Desmond tries like a polite curate to talk Sall out of her craziness, and then wonders why she asks at full volume, who the fuck is this?' I paused and looked hard at a photo of Desmond aged eight dressed as a beaming Red Indian. 'The point is if I treated Desmond with kid gloves, the way he treats old Sall, my son and I would be even further apart.'

Liz was looking at the same photograph. She stood up, walked across, examined it minutely, gave it a quick dusting and returned: 'Your son is another person, he is his own man, and he is not required to be anything like you. And, in any case, on this matter he might even be right. Personally I've no idea whether your approach is a useful therapeutic technique. I wonder, do the professionals, the doctors, care workers and so on, pretend to see Sall's phantoms as a way of helping her?'

'At least they let her eat trifle off the ground rather than force her to eat with a spoon! Dear old Desmond opines that it's unhygienic! Think old Sall gives a fuck about "hygiene" when her neural faculties are shot to buggery, Liz? Bloody hell, did Desmond himself never like to play in the dirt when he was a kid, or if he did, did he have wet wipes in his pocket to fend off the microbes? See that photograph up there? Was he lugging a pristine packet of Kleenex around him when he played at being a Comanche?'

There was a long pause while she stifled her resentment, then said she at any rate was going to contact him on his mobile once he'd got to Edinburgh. She'd apologise on her own behalf, but also on mine too if I wanted it. At that I fidgeted with the folded *Guardian*, made a meaningless noise, then swirled a glass of Kourtaki and said: 'There's another side to my tolerance of other people's hallucinations.'

I stared straight at her and she flushed, though without any apparent comprehension.

'Don't you remember? You recently informed me all about two extraordinary visions of your own.'

Her face showed signs of crumpling as she snapped, 'But I'm not mad, Joe. I'm not bloody deluded.'

'I agree. Not at all. Not even remotely. I believe your two extraordinary experiences entirely. I do not doubt you saw what you saw and experienced what you experienced.'

'I knew that you did. So why . . . ?'

'But understandably you've begged me to keep it a secret. It is not for public consumption for obvious reasons. Let's not mix things up, though. Your affair with Patrick Garnett is beside the point here. That's a secret as well, but it's a secret for very different reasons. If you'd had these visions without any Garnett in the picture, you would still have wished for an absolute discretion.'

'So would anyone . . .'

'Quite. No one wants to be thought crackers when in all other respects they are as sound as a pound. But let's just suppose you had told a man like Desmond all about your two visions?'

She scowled, and with a good deal of anger. 'You haven't been telling him anything? About my . . . visions . . . or about the other?'

'No,' I said, not entirely smoothly, as I recalled what I had almost let slip in cryptic code. 'But as sure as shot, Desmond would be very uncomfortable with those visions of yours, and he would laugh and try to talk you out of them. As of course would ninety-nine per cent of our friends, peers and fellow British citizens.'

'Well? So what are you saying?'

'That for authentic two-way communication one needs to learn the language of people whose experience is radically different from one's own. I try to understand and sympathise with my demented sister by listening to her madness rather than rejecting it. I try to understand your otherworldly experiences, which are certainly not mad, by listening to you and giving you credit. It's actually harder in your case because your two visions, which were both full of great revelatory beauty, took place in a context that is very painful for me. I genuinely believe that you had a glimpse of another and very beautiful world, but unfortunately you were embarked upon an affair with another man at the time. I'd have rather preferred . . .'

'Joe, I . . .'

'Let's drop it! There's a limit to how much I can stand to even think about it. But apropos today's events, people who only talk their own language, inflexible monoglots like Desmond, are not much help with the larger issues: Sickness, Sanity, Death, Bereavement, Faith, Love, Loss. They can stagger on fine pretending everything is under control through their forties, fifties and possibly sixties, but then it all catches up with them. Doesn't it, Liz? And by that stage, unfortunately, it's become too hard to learn any other language.'

Further instalment of *Galluses Galore*

Before he left the pub where he had been arguing with the drinkers about the events of 1982, Baggrow was unable to restrain his anger and disdain for these suddenly heartfelt patriots. One or two of them, as well as devoutly clipping on their braces and tossing away their belts, were still humming the National Anthem and recalling their country's martial splendour of twenty-five years ago. Their 1982 leader (*tyeufer than tungstin carbite, Madgie Thunder*), who had told them on the eve of war that they had the finest army, lived in the finest country, and would all soon demonstrate the finest unflagging heroism, was now being toasted in tearful retrospect, even by those who had once vehemently denounced her. Bewildered by such a welter of ironies, Baggrow was struck by the fact that these patriots were all real country folk, none of them urban (*ivvry yan a yakker, an nin ev them ard-edge cutting-hedge oorban ard knocks frae a busslin metoplis like Carel*). The patriotic Carlisle crowds of 1982 had been vociferously drunk in the Great Border City . . . whereas these folk were noisily drunk in a very remote country pub. Did this gentle and tender North Pennine landscape then do nothing to mitigate the tendency to mindless chauvinism, heroic warmongering, and a willingness to take back their braces as sign of willing servitude to those who knew best (*like a daft pyookin pudel garn back till its pyook*)?

Without any by your leave, Baggrow turned his back and walked angrily out of the pub. There were fading shouts of where you off, daft arse (*an sum gollert, rebel rooser! commnisht! hankist!, an yan er twa wid a lang memry shoots, Sittysun bliddy Smitt!*)? The object of their raucous insults decided to get on his bicycle and carry on back along the legendary A689 as if heading in the Carlisle direction. He realised that he had had enough of uphill propagandist tactics for the moment, and that in any case to start at the bottom is always inferior to starting at the top. To put it another way what was the point of trying to instil a new Weltanschauung (*feltchewin's an advanst way ev chewin away at hoo thoo can mek sense ev that dutty owd scrow cowd t'wurld*) in these front-saloon stalwarts, when their tabloid newspapers and the regular media pronouncements of disciplinarian premiers like Thomas Purley (*t'top gadger Tommy Pullet*) were urging them to be otherwise?

Had there been anyone to observe the last leg of his journey they would have been mighty impressed by the obscurity and arduousness of his itinerary (*Rainhard bliddy Fuchs might ev ed ter struggle ter foller Fenten on yon last lig*). Baggrow took a sly side route in the Eden Valley direction, then veered off down a remote C road, one which passed a couple of windblown ruined farms before turning into a pitted dirt track. The track continued up into the rugged foothills of the Pennines with an obvious sense of destination, as if it had once been excavated by the Water Board or other businesslike concern. However Baggrow did not ascend but took a left fork at that point, and beyond that a second left fork, so that he stayed resolutely on the flat, on the foothills of the foothills as it were. By now he had clocked up such a mileage he was starting to pant a little (*ee wuss swittin an puffin like a bliddy owd stim loco*). The beautiful but bare and melancholy landscape might aptly have been characterised as rather relentlessly stark (*like Tim Buck bliddy Twa*). The pitted track suddenly turned into a navigable stretch of lonning and after another half mile he was close to his destination. Ever and anon he would turn round as he cycled just to make sure he was unobserved, as if he wished to keep his precise where-abouts concealed at all costs. In fact, to teasingly give the game away, this journey into the heart of the Cumbrian Pennines, extolled across the world on tourist posters as England's Last Natural Wilderness (*aside frae mebbe t'Hooses ev Pallyment*) was connected with Baggrow's mindboggling revolutionary plans! He was on his way to do something that would: a) put a stop, he hoped, to this farcical belt and braces tyranny with all that it represented in the way of humiliating and insulting poor old Cumbrian manhood, and b) be a case of going straight to the power at the top rather than arsing about at the bottom (*an if yon isn't a sightspittin paranumberstick towtology er pleenazm, ah diven't know wat bliddy is*).

Baggrow stopped at the end of the track panting. He looked back along the route he'd taken, and saw that it was like a winding, snaking trail that, say, ancient invaders or miners might have taken to set about their necessary business (*batterin an flayin fwoak wid sords an lansis, er howkin awae at styan ter git at t'cwol*). In fact this trail led to nothing more dramatic than a sizeable fenced allotment, about an acre in all, one which Baggrow had been tending conscientiously for the last ten or so years. It had a couple of creosoted sheds, a handy tap and water barrel, neat vegetable beds where in season he grew potatoes, onions, leeks, carrots, virtually all the popular English vegetables other than celery which for some reason Baggrow loathed (*ee thowt sillry tyastit like shite wud an frankly ee saw neah point in gnashin awae at a stick ev bliddy shite*). About two hundred yards beyond his allotment at a slight elevation an overgrown path led to a ruined old farmhouse, last inhabited at a guess in the 1920s, meaning almost a century ago. The windows were all gone but the walls were solid enough and the roof had been repaired at some stage. Once a farmer had kept it for storage but now it was wholly deserted and abandoned. It certainly seemed ultra-emblematic of being this country's last natural wilderness (*aside frae t'Hooses ev Pallyment*), the last word in piquant dereliction. Which made it all the more perplexing that Baggrow walked with every lucid sign of definite purpose towards the ruined farm, as if intending to make a friendly if cautious social visit.

About a yard from the door as he stood in what had once been the front garden, he cupped his mouth and called out at discreet volume but in the broadest Cumbrian dialect imaginable, 'Are you there? It's me again! (*Sister, is thoo theer? Lookster, it's mesel, Fenten, hess laitit issel back ere agyan!*)

At which point there was a sudden moderately clamorous stirring within, something which evidently pleased Baggrow a great deal. For the first time that day he relaxed and smiled and began to hum a little happy song, one of those that have no lyrics worth mentioning but is pleasing nonetheless (*a bit like Feelit Mennlson's 'Sangs Wid Neah Wurds' an nin the wuss fer that, asser*).

Baggrow's mystery acquaintances gradually emerged, all blinking in the sunlight at this one who had hailed them. And if you had seen them that day, just as they were in all their pristine glory, you would assuredly have been well and truly thunderstruck (*thoo wud hev turrnt three shades ev pink an gollert, weel ah'll gah ter bliddy sea!*) . . .

8

Uncle Harrison was a passionate man and it was not only leeks and hound trails that stirred his countryman's blood. He was a fell farmer who was obliged to keep working dogs but he also liked dogs in general, in fact was completely daft about them, as was his wife Cissie who passed away six months before he did. His pet dogs caused him a good deal of work and anxiety as indeed do a lot of things one loves to distraction, e.g. spouses and children and one's chosen work or art or calling. No hard-pressed farmer could survive if he were sentimental about his sheepdogs, so it is difficult to explain why Harrison was quite so slavishly attentive to his far from glamorous mongrel Maisie, who made his remaining widowed months a sort of knockabout purgatory. Maisie herself was very old by then, in her mid-teens: a good bit deaf, poisonously and relentlessly flatulent, and likely to leave a bouquet of fresh turds on the mat every morning for her doting master who saw it as a touching and intelligible foible of old age rather than laziness. Perhaps Harrison could envisage the time when he too might not have iron control over his bowels and had decided to forgive himself unconditionally in advance. Yet for all her idleness and noisomeness, Maisie was impressively sage and inordinately wily when it came to food. In most respects she had no brains at all, but she certainly practised a strenuous ingenuity when it came to weaselling extra rations from her daft old boss.

I had no idea until Cora Dorr told me she had once taken her wayward dachshund Samson to visit a trainer that the proven way to iron out canine bad behaviour is by rewarding any good behaviour with food. This is not only a crude fatalistic homage to Pavlov but a sound evolutionary acknowledgement that the principal drive in a dog's constitution, historically and since the birth of time, is the drive to stuff its face. In case you think this a bald and gratuitous digression, let me point out that I make a living of sorts by writing cookery books and stuffing gourmet vegetarian grub down the necks of punters who are prepared to sit down and write a bloody essay just to get their hands upon my exquisite food. While you're at it, ask anyone who has ever starved for more than a day precisely what it's like in obsessional and cognitive, never mind physiological, terms, and they'll tell you all they can think about is imaginary, hallucinatory and maddening food, the tantalising thing that turns the world around.

A precise account of Maisie's senile demandingness is a rather elaborate matter. In her last regal years she suddenly took a great liking to guzzling cat treats (2 for a 1) which once upon a time I think were also called cat nips (2 for a 1 also, though what the hell 'nip' represents is anybody's guess). Luckily for her, Harrison's cat Simone (I do not lie, that was old Cissie's quaintly continental notion, and they also had a goldfish called Pierre) wasn't particularly interested in these dried treats, neither the tuna and prawn flavour nor the bilious-sounding turkey and duck. But Maisie loved all cat nip varieties to distraction, in due deference to which newly widowed Harrison would give her a handful every time he got her back in the farmhouse from a walk. He was, so he believed, intelligently rewarding her for her good behaviour, obediently coming home that is, by acknowledging her principal evolutionary drive. And although Harrison didn't exactly celebrate Maisie's unique genius by renaming his farmhouse 1 Evolutionary Drive, Mallstown, North Cumbria, he might as well have . . .

'Guid lass! Wat a canny owd beast thoo is, Maze.'

She soon discovered that following Harrison outside to

peg the washing out, which took a cursory five minutes, then waddling back inside immediately after him, constituted an obedient returning-back-into-the-house. She stared at Harrison with anticipatory saliva once they were back in the kitchen and he was boiling the kettle for his tea. Harrison, fool that he was, guffawed at her cuteness, called her a crafty old bitch (how very true!) and dealt her a generous handful of cat nips. And that, of course, was the end of any easy life for octogenarian Harrison. Before long Maisie extrapolated the rules to such an extent that if he let her out for a pee she would take ten seconds to do nothing whatever, then bark long and deafeningly to be allowed back in. Once inside after her ten-second outing, she would salivate for more cat nips. If Harrison didn't give her them very soon, she would keep on barking hysterically till he did. Then showing signs of needing to piss after all, she would whine by the door so that he was obliged to let her out in case she irrigated the hall. Once more she would lounge outside, counting rapidly to twenty, and then bark to be let in for more nips. On a good day this might happen up to ten times an hour during the Sunday afternoon omnibus repeat of *Coronation Street*, Harrison's favourite television drama. With all that up and down cat-nipping (a very accurate verb) Harrison's arse barely touched the sofa, and he damn soon lost the plot with Corrie just as he was losing the plot with Maisie . . .

He shared this escalating problem of who was doing what with whom, with his panting old oppressor, pointing sadly at the television screen: 'A thowt yon skinny laddo theer wuss courtin wid that big skoppin body theer, Maze. But it turns oot she's a secret wassacomie Lesbun . . . an ah'd misst aw that wid thee barkin like ell at t'back dooer.'

You have not heard the half of it. The reason why Harrison had to watch the omnibus repeat, and theoretically choke as it were on a surfeit of dramatic tension across five continuous episodes, was because his dog Maisie would not permit him stay up to see the early evening weekday ones. Cissie in her last invalid months had favoured going to bed very early, at about half past seven, which given that she still rose at six every day was reasonable enough (she used to watch the Corrie teatime omnibus to compensate, just as reciprocally, and like a fearless grown-up, Harrison had stayed up watching the telly as long as he liked). However when it came to loyalty, Maisie had always been Cissie's dog more than Harrison's, so that when her mistress went to bed early, so did her shadow of a dog, who trotted behind her and slept on the covers.

'Budge up, Maze,' she would tenderly complain. 'Thoo's got aw t'covers and thoo's got me pinnt ter t'wo, wid thee greet paws stritched oot an vanya in me fyass!'

Once Cissie died, Maisie saw no reason for change in a welcome routine, or for Cissie's husband to depart from the classic pattern. Thus at half past seven on Corrie nights, Monday, Wednesday, Friday and Sunday, Maisie would sit at the bottom of the staircase and bark impatiently to go upstairs to her favourite bed. The first time this happened, not realising that he was part of the equation, Harrison opened the door and let her trot upstairs, then watched her turn half way up, leer down accusingly and bark like hell for him to follow on. By dint of puzzled trial and error, and Pavlovian responding to Maisie's admonishing barks, Harrison eventually learnt that he too was required to go to bed at seven thirty. He too was obliged to get inside it, whether he liked it or not, and have Maisie squatting on the top like a malodorous and loudly snoring walrus. He was to be Cissie's inadequate bedfellow replacement, and if he tried sneaking out of it bolt awake as he was, this cat-nip-daft (an ext. that is 3 about 2 for 1) walrus would turn and whine, bark, woof and rant at him for leaving her alone in his faithless and inexplicable desire to be a night owl (ext. like a 2 of 1) . . .

Mongrel Maisie simply could not sleep on her own, you

see, in advanced old age. She had to have company which also must lie motionless and go to sleep, no matter that Harrison was wide awake in the bright twilight and would be up at five next morning as a result. In some ways it reads like the onset of dementia in the mongrel, not the man, and yet as far as I know the condition is unknown in any other animal species.

As crucial coda I do not wish to overlook Maisie's original habit of a kind of mineral treading, a species of grape-harvest stamping, which she took to in that final spring. In Harrison's last few months it happened to be an early and beautiful springtime and the swallows were nesting in the disused barn which he used as a handy coalhouse. The coalhouse door had to be left open all the time for the swallows to get in and out, for nothing is sadder than the sight of a dead swallow which has vainly sought for an exit before dropping in exhaustion to the ground below. None of which presented any problem until Maisie's progressive dementia took an unfathomable turn. When Harrison let her out for a pee just before his premature bedtime, she took to wandering in and out of the coalhouse and, worse, somnambulistically padding up and down the mound of coal itself so that her paws became indescribably black and filthy. Harrison, who had over eighty years of exhaustive animal husbandry under his belt, had no idea why this one beast should develop the insane habit of coal treading, as if she were trying to flail her way to a mountain summit to prove an elusive point.

He bawled amazed: 'Wat's ah ganna dyeuh wid a body like thee? Thoo hess me bliddy beat wid thee pezzlin t'bliddy cwol eap!'

The first time she did it Harrison didn't notice till she was back inside with her height-of-fashion wellington boots, and his spruce old sitting room was suddenly like a dirty railway coal depot. He had to drag her outside and wash her paws in a bowl of water, then dry her off and soothe her with quadruple cat nips. The torment of the cascading situation was suddenly vivid in his mind. If he closed the coalhouse door to stop Maisie treading the coal, he would imprison and distress the swallows. Unwilling to suffocate and starve the little birds, neither could he let Maisie out unattended, for she would go a-gleeful coal-treading and turn his house into an extended pitheap (a 2 outside of or extracted from a 1). Which meant he could either close the coalhouse door for a short and secure interval while Maisie was peeing in the yard . . . or risk her going out on her own and hope she'd neglect to go grape treading. Assuming the former, he was seriously worried he'd forget to reopen the coalhouse before ushering her back inside the house. A third really dull and dispiriting option was to put her on the lead every single time she wanted out, and to saunter out there with her in all weathers to prevent any coalhouse invasion. Luckily as it turned out Harrison passed away before the tormenting limitations of all the dog and swallow and coalhouse options finally drove him mad.

Understand that Harrison's dogly subjugation is not being described here by way of random local colour. Instead he is an important paradigm for all of us, inasmuch as he had a certain hoped-for vision of his future, in this case his final months, instead of which he got what he got. He got comprehensive domination by an old mongrel, one who never looked in the mirror, and humbly said to herself that perhaps she was not striking enough in looks, brains or pedigree to be a tyrant or a domineering princess. No doubt Harrison always hoped that Cissie and he would have another ten years together rapt in evening *Corrie*-watching, instead of which it was loony old, wily old Maisie who finally called the shots after Cissie's death. What we are talking about is the gap between one's dreams and what one gets, an instructive universal if ever there was. I

143

for example hoped to be a money-making cookery writer, but instead I have had the sporadic acclaim and not the lucre. I had also sincerely hoped for the same easy-going marital felicity in my seventies as I had in all earlier decades. But no, it was not to be . . .

What do we call this thing that is beyond our control? Some call it Destiny but I am not a fatalist and instead I would call it Time and Chance, an altogether less constrictive and reductive model. Others would say that Time and Chance is just another way of saying the Hand of God, which is where Elizabeth Gladstone might have to square her recent visions with her recent deeds. In my lucid moments I think she was meant to have those visions of the beyond, that they were her unique and instructive privilege as she embarked on her eighth decade. I do not think they were necessarily meant to come about via dance-hall infidelity but then I am not the one who ordains the business of Time and Chance, am I?

It was 1945 and I was ten years old before I made the linguistic distinction between my favourite sister Mary and the dialect word *sister*. I did not know till then it was usually written as *sista* and is a contraction of *sees ter?*, meaning d'you see?, or see ye/look ye! I don't mean I thought that my sister and the verb 'to see' were the same thing, but I took it for granted that the superior dialect had cheekily parodied or stolen a respectable but inferior English word for itself. Another example would be year as *ear* in dialect. In fact this is merely a case of idle abbreviation or elision, where the dialect speaker cannot be bothered to say the initial y. But as a child I had a picture of years as a string of lugholes, so that when someone talked about *twenny ear sen*, meaning twenty years since, I had an image of twenty bulbous lugs marking the passage of two unimaginable decades, i.e. twice my age. Much later as a Fifties student the word *vanya* or *va'neah*, meaning nearly or almost, made me naturally enough think of Chekhov and his *Uncle Vanya*. On some sleepy subliminal level I vaguely felt that Uncle Vanya had a parallel existence where he spoke Cumbrian dialect, a nonsensical extrapolation if ever there was. Nevertheless there he had a uniquely surreal private life where unbeknownst to other characters in the play he communed with himself buffoonishly in an unintelligible and preposterous English dialect.

A lot of this muddying of fact and fantasy is down to orthography. Some of the old-guard enthusiasts will stoutly insist that there is only one way to represent the dialect vowels, their own superior way, and will shower them with meaningless accents corresponding to no known linguistic convention. 'Face' for example can be written as *fyass*, *fias* or *féace*, the last one with its pointless accent over the Nordic diphthong. They are all as valid on the page as each other, despite the stridency of the partisan experts, if only because a dialect is not a language, it is only a bloody dialect! A dialect might have a literature and in the case of Cumbrian it is venerable and immense. But one cannot prescribe for it a final orthography, at best one can only subject it to a universal phonetic convention, and only squint-eyed linguistics professors will be able to read the bloody stuff at that stage.

What am I saying? If at ten I had pictured the word as *sista* instead of *sister*, and *dista?* (do you?) instead of *duster?*, I would not have imagined Mary and a cloth duster as picturesque emblems of the verbs 'to see' and 'to do'. This partly explains why in my fable *Galluses Galore* I pun so idiotically and to the nth. Because the language I am writing in has no proper linguistic conventions, I can do what I bloody well like with it, and make it pun sideways, longways, arseways and more! The point being that all of our adult minds work on two levels, the adult rational and the infant pictorial, and no matter how hard you try you cannot erase the tendency to fit a child's picture to the sound pattern of a word.

By way of relevant illustration, when Desmond Gladstone was three years old in 1963, Liz, who has always been a folk music enthusiast, would regularly sing him to sleep with an old English ditty that starts, *My father's a hedger and ditcher* . . .

Infant soprano Desmond would soon join in the infectious song, and would render his own innocent pictorial version of the same line: '*My father's a hedgehog and* . . .'

At which I find myself sighing more deeply than I care to sigh. How true that was in retrospect. A prickly old porcupine more like . . .

Menu of South American banquet served at The Lonning, 8 p.m., 9 December 2008

Maças recheadas a la Señhor Zeziñho Gladstone
(Brazilian savoury stuffed apples. Best quality eating apples stuffed with kidney beans mixed with cumin, chillis, cream and lime juice, then topped with fried cashews. Slow baked in a medium oven to stop the apples splitting)

Cacerola de berenjana
(Nicaraguan aubergine casserole. Fried aubergines soaked in an incendiary and very rich sauce and covered with cheese. For the sauce green peppers, onion and garlic are fried together, an incontinent quantity of diluted tomato purée added, together with chilli peppers and a discreet dash of that top-heavy vandal of a spice, allspice. Place aubergines and sauce in alternating layers in a casserole, top with a copious blanket of pungent *queso*, then bake it till it sizzles, rasps and sings at you)

146

Hongos in salsa verde
(In a blender whirl together green Mexican tomatillos with garlic and cumin. Pour this over your mushrooms that you have fried with onions and chilli peppers, then cover and cook for a meditative quarter hour. The pungent green tomatoes in combination with the fiery chillis will leave their unapologetic mark on your memory, though hopefully not on your underwear. Hah!)

I also spoiled my guests with a delirious Guatemalan recipe of zucchini stuffed with corn, cream and cheese, and made an Argentinian salad of garden spinach and apple with a lime juice dressing. In addition to tortillas and the like, I threw at them that Mexican rice dish *arroz verde*, which boggles the eyes as much as it boggles everything else. You blister and blacken onions, garlic, chillis and green peppers under a grill, then churn all that in a blender along with cilantro, parsley, shredded lettuce and a little water. The dry rice which has been fried in olive oil is covered with this delightful pondweed green liquor, then simmered pilau-style in a covered pan. Once the *arroz* is done it is generously seasoned, the cover replaced, and it is allowed to stand and ponder its future for some fifteen minutes. The finished rice looks like lush green tender tillage and the taste is out of this world, right enough.

Cooking rice in a closed pan in a precise quantity of necessary liquid is a mature art and not for footlers or novices. Suffice to say the making of the best Persian pollo with its saffron and its steaming under tea towel lids etc. demands more patience, exactitude and love than most of us have in our lazy occidental bosoms. Apropos the Mexican *arroz verde*, Cora Dorr, gurgling enchantedly, said it certainly tasted as if it was made with love, but added that an exhausting job doesn't help when it comes to taking one's time as a chef. Bill Pargeter in a sweating trance with the astringent *hongos*, and obviously enjoying

147

the tussle with the blazing fire inside his mouth and mind . . . suddenly came out with a stark non-sequitur.

'But what do we do with all of them? Do we keep them all in zoos?'

It was only yesterday that Desmond and I had visited Sall, and for a mad moment I thought he was talking about the old and demented. Should we keep all the elderly confused in zoos? I was about to point out that actually security-coded doors are about stopping old demented absconders from being run over by lorries or tormented by kids, in which respect they were subtly different from locked animal cages, when Marjorie Staff made the connection.

'He means cows and sheep. He means that if we all went vegetarian we would need to do something with the cows and sheep. Isn't that what you mean?'

I sniffed. 'Simple. We keep them as pets. We domesticate them, so that after a little practice we're able to take our obedient old cow down the road for a walk. Likewise we train a domestic sheep not to shit on the carpet and invite it inside to watch the six o'clock news.'

'Ha,' snorted Cora Dorr.

'Oh come on,' I said. 'Where's your imagination? Or as Bill seems to be suggesting, we consider the countryside to be a new type of open-plan zoo. A cage-free mega-zoo where the sheep and cows roam unhindered. And before you ask why would the farmers bother to look after them when they can't turn them into meat, I say we pay the farmers not to kill them. Pay the farmers to let the sheep and cows have a grand life and die of peaceful natural causes. We can easily afford it, because we'll have so much more money once all the butchers are closed down, and we don't have to whack out a fortune on meat.'

Marjorie said, 'What'll happen to all the unemployed butchers?'

'Retrain them as greengrocers. We'll need lots more of

those once we've closed down all the butchers' shops. Slaughterhouse workers ditto. Though frankly, anyone who can do that kind of revolting job might need more than a little genteel career counselling and retraining.'

William Dixon wiped some stray cilantro from his mouth and said: 'There's nothing wrong in wanting the moon I suppose.'

'Spot on, parson. Sorry. No you're right, inasmuch as I get so sick of arguing logically all the time. Meat eaters are incorrigible and are never going to change, not unless they develop lethal cholesterol levels and think it might just save their lives. So given their rock-solid obstinacy, what's the point of talking sense? I might as well talk pie in the sky. I'm not going to hurt anyone, am I?'

Cora said, 'The world can't all eat meat, even if it wanted to. Only the relatively rich can eat meat. And the newly rich can't get enough of it. In these so-called tiger economies, the young Chinese and Indian couples who suddenly have disposable incomes are stuffing themselves with meat seven days a week. It used to be a monthly treat and now it is the norm.'

'But do they suffer?' asked Pargeter. 'Do they feel anything much?'

Again it was guesswork whether he meant the meat-obsessed young tiger-economy couples getting searing indigestion with their new diet, or the very poorest people across the globe who would be even poorer now with world prices shooting up as a result of the tigerish young couples' new diet, or . . .

'He means the cows and sheep again,' said Marjorie. 'I'm sure that's what he means. Because you were talking about slaughterhouses . . .'

I sighed. 'Those people who seriously doubt whether animals feel pain, many of them scientists and philosophers, should learn a little science and a little philosophy. Forget about foxes being torn to pieces by dogs, and why bother

149

to dispute idiotic words like 'painless' and 'instantaneous'? Though just consider. Would a terminally ill fox hunter consent to be ripped to shreds by his beloved hounds, assuming it were so completely painless and so instantaneous? Surely he should willingly agree to it if he wants to put his money where his mouth is. But let's be less dramatic. If I stand on my dog's toe, it screeches in pain. QED. Squealing like a stuck pig speaks for itself, hein? Maybe sheep are quiet to the point of mute about their suffering but they still damn well feel it. The stun gun and the bolt to the brain are not instantaneous, nor is the ride in the lorry to the slaughterhouse without dismal distress and suffering. Only one in a thousand meat eaters would volunteer to work in a slaughterhouse because they would be as sick as a dog after five disgusting minutes. Bugger it, it makes me ill to think about it, which is why I talk my ad hoc nonsense for preference.'

I omitted to say that Liz wasn't there eating South American but was out at a gala quiz night at the nearby pub. The quiz was to raise funds for a new parish hall kitchen and as half our acquaintances would be there, there was no chance she could be up to something covert and deceitful. Believe me, logic and reason had nothing to do with it, I was still as insecure and jealous as a jilted teenager. When she got back just after eleven, she told me how she'd excelled to general acclaim with the names and dates of Beatles songs and the political events of the Fifties. But the snowball tie question was absolutely impossible, even for a Regius Professor of Geography. How many islands were there in the Indonesian archipelago? She couldn't recall the correct answer but assuming it had been, say, 14,735, many of them no doubt bare rocks with a handful of sheep on them, anything more than plus or minus fifty was not even in the running.

I looked at her a little tensely over our glasses of Chilean red, and she smiled, took a deep breath and asked: 'How are you tonight? Are you alright?'

I stiffened a little. 'Eh? I think so. A little enflamed from the Grade A Mexican chillis but otherwise . . .'

'I meant in the light of you know what.'

'Oh, I see. In that case the most accurate answer is up and down. In fact very up and very down. Some days oddly find me quite oblivious of recent history, as if it had never happened. Other days it bores away at me like an ache or a twinge, or a trapped bloody nerve. There's a finite time you see in which . . .'

'It was just I wondered if that horrible row with Desmond . . .'

'What about it?'

'If it's connected. If it's because you're a bit out of sorts . . .'

I restrained a gasp. 'You make me sound like a toothing toddler. Instead of which I'm a fucking cuck . . . I'm actually a hoodwinked septuagenarian.'

'Oh hell, I don't want to stir it up. But . . .'

'The two things are discrete and distinct, I promise you. I am very raw at times from what happened with you and Garnett, that is one thing. I get shirty sometimes with my son who is so different from me, that is another. But how can I put it? Sometimes you see someone who has been celebrating their birthday at home in boozy fashion set off for the pub to put away even more. You could say they are starting out for the pub in a condition in which most people leave it. Well facing up to a partner's infidelity in one's twilight years has the same sort of hang on, hang on feel about it. Hang on, hang on! you say to yourself. Shouldn't it be 1975 that she started a-roaming, not 2005? Sometimes I say to myself rather frantically, how the hell am I supposed to bounce back, when at seventy-three I can't even bounce forwards or sideways? It is considerably harder to lick one's wounds at the end of one's days and . . .'

'The end? But you are as fit as a fluke. You might well have another twenty-five years.'

'Here's hoping. At any rate, I would feel the twinges from my wounds irrespective of Desmond saying the wrong thing at the wrong time. To be honest, it was the sight of my sister Sall with her brain like a plate of scrambled eggs that made me so surly with him. He is all full steam and go ahead, and Sall is all no steam and going bloody nowhere. The trouble is I can vividly remember Sall being in her right mind, because it was only three damn years ago. Sometimes I even picture the old sane Sall peering into the future and looking at this new Sall and it breaking her heart, this unbearable vision of what she will be. Just supposing. Imagine she'd been down on her hols staying with nephew Des in Wilts in 2005. I wonder whether one of his crowd-pulling clairvoyants would have foreseen and told her the same thing? In 2005 there was the sane Sall, call that version S to represent her age, whereas now we have S plus 3, and S plus 3 needs total care because her short-term memory is completely done for. With a struggle and if I flap my arms and tease her, she recognises kid brother Joe. But if I talk about you and any of her friends, I have to give her lots of clues and say everything ten times before she gets it.'

Liz said, 'Desmond saw all that as well, and he was upset too.'

I sniffed. 'And yet he kept his safe distance. Just like they all keep their bloody distance.'

'Who does?'

'It's a pathetic cliché, but it's still the truth. Lose your marbles in regal style, start talking word salad and not being able to go to the bog on your own, and guess what? One by one your friends will stop their visits, while long before that most of your doting relatives have thrown in the towel. After all, it's not as if her care home isn't central. It's right in the middle of her village, it lies on a thoroughfare, and is a short cut to the shops. Dozens of her old mates pass by it fifty times a week and precisely two of them go in to see her. Challenge those who don't, and you know what they say?'

'I can guess.'

'That it upsets them too much! It upsets them what she's become! It upsets them to see her jabbering to herself and eating trifle with her ear and having visions of folk who died fifty years ago. Bah. What do you think is an appropriate answer to that one, Liz? Well stone the crows and fuck me gently, is mine! Fuck me gently, dear friends and dear family, and 'tis sorry I am that you be so turrible upset by that repugnant old wreck in the corner.'

She stood up restlessly. 'You are too harsh.'

'I disagree. I'm not harsh enough I promise you. In any case senile dementia is a bit like sexual abuse or breast cancer . . . it is a modern epidemic, not a rarity. If it doesn't get you now, it'll get you or your best pal or your best pal's brother or sister next year or the year after that, or the year after that. And if everyone concerned gives up on everyone else, because it makes them so upset, it means the whole bloody world will soon be giving up on everyone else ad infinitum.'

I paused as something else intimately related to old age and not losing one's grip, viz. a comfortable and secure annual income, came embarrassingly to mind.

'I am working like a dog at this dialect competition you know. You would think I was trying to write fucking *Sense and Sensibility* I do so much crossing out and starting again and then starting again until I think I'm climbing the walls. After all this bloody slog, if my entry doesn't win the £50,000, there is no damn justice.' I winced and turned a good bit sheepish. 'That prize money by the way will all be yours if I win.'

She looked considerably startled. She even made an odd little gasping noise. 'All mine?'

'Yes. I have foolishly pissed away most of Harrison's legacy as Desmond rightly observes. Meaning well past retirement age you are still obliged to keep on grafting away as interior designer. Morally, it's the least I can do. In fact morals are everything right now. Morally, I ought to win the bloody competition and morally you ought to have the bloody money. Morally, I should ring up before long and apologise to Desmond. In fact I think I will right away. The only obstacle now is . . .'

'What?'

'Time and Chance. Or maybe not. Maybe it's on my side after all.'

9

Further instalment of *Galluses Galore*

Observe a most puzzling sight (*lookster t'cut on yon*). Clad in some borrowed West Cumberland Farmers wellies, Thomas Purley, the government leader, no less (*t'varra syam Tommy Pullet, an nut iss twin brudder*) was slowly progressing along a remote Pennine dirt road. He was in the company of four of his burly security men as well as a local chap Fenton Baggrow, who for the one and only time in his life was wearing not only a pair of braces but a handsome linen suit. This striking and picturesque group were all striding out on foot, there was not a quad bike or Japanese four-wheel drive to be seen, much less the customary ministerial motorcade which would not of course have relished a terrain such as this. Equally as surprising, in addition to an absence of national TV crews and national journalists, there was no entourage of regional journalists or local officials accompanying this small and highly focused group. It was a balmy spring day in March 2018 with a bracing quantity of sunshine and only the lightest of refreshing breezes. Nevertheless and despite the minimum ten to maximum twenty pieces of fresh fruit or vegetable the premier willingly consumed each day, he found himself puffing with the exertion.

The premier (*t'top gadger*) did not of course think he was in the company of a devious Cumbrian rabble-rouser called Baggrow; in fact he thought quite the opposite. He believed himself to be walking beside a new breed of provincial entrepreneur, a mega-market garden magnate called Jackson Holiday; someone who had taken an intel-ligent leaf (*is this ganna be a bare-fyasst misht mettyfer?*) out of the book of one or two horticulture magnates in the south of England. There of course all these things tended to be more de facto feasible (*cos t'suth is where it's aw at, and t'noth is where it bliddy isn't*). Not only that but this Jackson Holiday had an admirable and subtle fashion sense and the braces he was wearing, visible underneath his graceful linen jacket, were of a costly connoisseur variety, maroon and gold in colour and imported from a four-generations family factory in Tennessee (*Owd Hank Highbury's Hang 'Em High an Twang 'Em Low Classick Galluses*).

A month ago Jackson Holiday had written a devout and humble letter to Thomas Purley explaining that he was successfully engaged in developing an innovative if not ground-breaking (*anudder varra poorall pun*) fruit and vegetable mega-concern in a remote but beautiful part of the Cumbrian Pennines. Using solar panels, unique hydroponic cultivation systems, a new type of US university-devised greenhouse complex vast in size and horticultural vision, Holiday was cultivating the first ever strains of luscious Cumbrian melons, mouthwatering Cumbrian oranges, pungent North Pennine lemons, England's Last Natural Wilderness green, red, yellow and orange peppers, succulent Cumbrian eggplants, and there were even plans to try out Cumbrian mangoes and Cumbrian coconuts. All this of course in addition to the usual potatoes, onions, root vegetables and other quotidian North English fare. And not only was the JH fruit and veg mega-market garden a vibrant concern after only a year in operation, it was also a seedbed in terms of industrial relations vis-a-vis its ten employees. In a nutshell, Premier Purley, it is only not a seedbed but a hotbed of your own old-fashioned and time-sanctioned values! In a further nutshell, as well as a seedbed and a hotbed, it is another kind of metaphorical bed, as yet not defined though it indubitably exists. Firstly, all ten men who work there, in obedience to managerial policy, must wear conspicuous braces while they are going about their horticultural labours, some of them very arduous, as a sign that hard work and a proper concern for one's personal appearance need not be mutually exclusive. Secondly, in addition to their willing adherence to the braces which, truth be told, occasionally get ever so minutely in the way of some of the struggles with the more junglish greenhouse vegetations (*a cripper er leanna er liffy horkit can sumtimes git tangelt up in their galluses so they ev ter feyt ter hextricet theirsels frae its amrus clutshis*), the JH employees must also wear a smart suit and tie at all times (*ter show their eekerly dappur galluses ter mowst fetchin effect*) . . .

'Good Lord,' said Thomas Purley in amazement at his London desk. 'Compulsory suits and ties? They've done more than I ask. They've gone beyond what is required! Their values are so old-fashioned I believe my dear old mother if she were alive would salute them and whisk out the celebratory seed cake and press second and third and fourth portions on those suited heroes!'

The suits and ties Jackson Holiday had explained were both imported from a family factory in Switzerland and made of a special and very expensive material. This secret formula fabric had a unique frictional and electrostatic property that amazingly repelled all dust, all moisture and all dirt consequent on even the most strenuous of horticultural labours, including even the notorious digging format known as bastard trenching (*bastud bliddy trenshin, an a reet bliddy bastud it is!*). Plus it also repelled all chemicals, all paint and every other possible incidental besmirchment. Would you believe the things these quiet and understated Swiss were so capable of?

'It's because the Swiss, par excellence, have hitherto had the European monopoly on old-fashioned values!'

exclaimed the premier at his metropolitan desk (*gollers t'top gadger aw thrillt ter bits in his swiffle chur in Lunnon*). 'Everything devolved to cantons. Keep at a respectable distance what you think might sully the body politic. Eat plenty of cheese. Up in the Alps the Alpine fresh fruit and vegetables are of course a by-word.'

Not only that, but the Swiss suit material was self-regulatingly thermostatic (*anudder laffable pleeanazm, asser*). It was delightfully warm and cosy in winter, when the frosts were most cruel on the market garden's vegetable rows. Likewise it was refreshingly cool in summer when the employees were required to dally in boiling hot equatorial greenhouses attending to the Cumbrian lemons, oranges, pineapples and guavas. What that meant was it was more than possible as a JH worker to do one's honest toil in suit and tie and braces (*neah broon cwots er grubby owd overalls fer these dappur marraboys*), effectively turning a blue-collar job into a white-collar job, and effectively endorsing that a smart and sound outer man reflects a smart and sound inner man. Beyond that, and even more important, a smart and sound and responsible and disciplined modern citizen with a capital MC! It was a testament to Purleyism (*pollytickle doctorin Pullet-style!*), a bold Purleyan (*Pullet-style!*) innovation in industrial relations. The proof of the pudding was obvious, inasmuch as all the JH men arrived whistling to work every morning, more or less after the manner of Snow White and her seven dwarves, though admittedly minus any Snow White and in fact every one of the ten JH gardeners was well over five foot eight (*ivvry yan ev them natty owd gardners in their luffly syeuts wuss a skoppin greet sconcer*).

In his letter Jackson Holiday had begged the premier (*t'top gadger*) to make a special brief diversion from his imminent Cumbrian itinerary, just to come and see his Purleyan principles in action in this beautiful country setting. His security entourage must accompany him of course, but please could they dispense with the national and local journalists and TV crews, could they please be requested to stay at the bottom on the main road? One old-fashioned value both of them obviously shared, Thomas Purley and his entrepreneurial disciple JH, was personal modesty, and likewise the ten horticultural employees were men who preferred sober hard work and getting their heads down to beaming for mugshots in the national and local presses.

The premier, continued Holiday, need only take a half an hour out of his itinerary to see not only his values in action as it were, but something even more down to earth (*sek a varra atless pun*). For here at the JH mega-gardens was a regional enterprise that was doing its very best to make the life-saving five pieces of fresh fruit and vegetables easier and cheaper for the locals to get hold of. It was also of course at the forthright cutting edge in terms of offering them a wider range and choice.

'Good. Good, good. Cutting edge. Range and choice! Ha! Just like schools, the media, the NHS (*Natnal Helth Surfers*) and . . . and . . . haberdashery and millinery and . . . kissagrams and chimney sweeps, if ever I get the chance.'

For JH, according to his letter, obviously offered more than good old-fashioned Cumbrian taties, peas, parsnips, cabbage and carrots to name but five life-saving pieces. It also offered sleek new-fashioned Cumbrian capsicums (*where the ell did thoo git thee grade fower CSE in Lating? Soorly thoo reetly means 'capsica'?*), eggplants, chayotes, yams, drumsticks, lauki, jackfruit and physillis (*a forren fryeut nyam nut ter be bowdily spyeunerised, asser*).

Amazingly JH's offer had been readily acceded to, and we must give Thomas Purley credit (*aw kridit ter Tommy Pullet!*), that instead of having it roundly vetted and disapproved by a hundred civil servants and minders, he simply kept mum about his special meeting with Holiday until the time arrived. Five minutes before he and his entourage were due to drive on to inspect a sausage-factory expansion in

Carlisle, the premier briskly told everyone in the motorcade what was what, this was what was going to happen, no fussing and no gratuitous backchat. He dragged his four startled minders a hundred yards up the deserted D road where, right enough, Jackson Holiday was waving at them and clutching a handsome presentation box of Cumbrian pineapples and Cumbrian pomegranates, and some smart WCF wellies for the premier. JH put the present down by the roadside to collect on their return, and watched admiringly as the premier (*t'top gadger*) shuffled on his wellies. Ten minutes later here they were within sight of Baggrow's allotment, and beyond that the rugged ruined farmhouse. Premier Purley gazed hopefully if a little worriedly at both (*Tommy Pullet wuss ivver seah sleetly tyan aback*), but luckily for Baggrow the ancient hedge surrounding his one acre (*yah yakker*) allotment was just high enough to have concealed a notional state-of-the-art greenhouse complex.

At this point JH hurriedly begged the party to wait where they were and he would bring his ten employees out to meet them. He promised they would be clutching for inspection some sample Cumbrian coconuts and paradigm voluptuous Cumbrian passion fruit, and the security men and their charge licked their lips in anticipation.

Baggrow walked up quickly to the hedge and peered through the high bolted gate. Then he called out something in what might have been Mandarin Chinese as far as the London visitors were concerned. He spoke possibly two sentences and the visiting party smiled amused, assuming perhaps some of the JH workers were Bulgarians or Slovaks with their quaint sounding Mandarin-type languages. After about a minute the gate was slowly opened and an extremely peculiar and definitely frightening group of people walked through it in a sober and dignified procession. Premier Purley was shocked out of his wits, it is true to say, and even the hardboiled security chaps were seized with a kind of temporary and partial rigor mortis (*they were flait bliddy richard and stud theer flummoxt wid their gobs white oppen).* Instead of the expected ten JH horticulturalists there were only five, and not only was JH's simple arithmetic all to pot, if he thought these folk were the type to employ in his mega-market garden, he was as gullible as they come.

'What?' gasped Thomas Purley, and his speech came out with considerable difficulty. 'But who on earth are these extraordinary people? And why does the very sight of them literally petrify every one of my faculties?'

Fenton Baggrow turned round from businesslike conferring with his charges and said to him: 'But you've still got speech haven't you, Premier? You've got vision. You've got hearing. As a responsible politician, what more could you possibly want *(duster mebbe wannt t' uth an stars as weel)?*'

'Eh? Well motor locomotion wouldn't be a bad thing. Especially for these security men as well. They're as frozen stiff and immobile as I am. Frankly they're not a lot of use to me in the security sense if they can't stroll from A to B, Mr Holiday.'

'True enough,' concurred Baggrow. 'But the main thing to remember, sir, is that no one here is going to do you any serious harm. Nor will they harm your immobile security men, I promise. Now then. Can you guess what my personal motto is?'

His interlocutor in the wellies ruminated for no more than a second. 'Oddly enough I think I can. According to the letter you wrote, your motto is "All Things Purleyan Are Fine By Me" *(ah gah alang wid ivvrythin Pullet-style when it comes ter soond an doon till uth pollyticks).*'

'I was lying,' sighed Baggrow.

'Oh?' sighed Thomas Purley in a rather different timbre *(Pullet sight wid raither mare of a wirry owd metapulletin sigh).*

'No, my real motto is something else. It's, *Neah Badness! Neah Minness!* That's it in the local dialect, at any rate.'

'Eh? And what does that mean in good old-fashioned English?'

'It means, "No Badness! No Meanness!". If I was to make it a bit longer it would also say, "I wouldn't harm a fly". But that would be too long for a succinct motto, so I always leave the last bit out.'

Still very uneasy at the fact his limbs were frozen solid, Purley said: 'And what about these incredible folk? Who are they? What are they? I swear I've never seen anything like them in all my born days. (*Nivver in my born daze chutters Pullet hev ah seen owt like yon. Nivver awivver awoor!*)'

'I will explain,' said Baggrow in a dispassionate but reasonably amiable tone. 'I will explain to you just exactly who they are.'

End of instalment of *Galluses Galore*

My Uncle Harrison believed some laughable and extraordinary things, though, be honest, who do you know who doesn't have their ridiculous beliefs? A few dauntless political celebrities for a start, but there is no point in making cheap and redundant satire at this non-dialect point in the story. For example Harrison swore that when laying a coal fire one must draw the curtains to keep out strong sunlight, which will put out a fire in its early stages. I mocked him roundly and proceeded to lay his fire on this bright and brilliant March morning, and pulled back his curtains until both of us as well as the fire were blinded by each other's radiance, as it were. The fire took off and crackled away merrily even though we could barely see it for its dancing patina of sunlight. Harrison sniffed and said that was a one in a hundred fluke and demanded I try again. I pointed out that I would have to put the blazing fire out with a blanket or a soda siphon before I could lay the bugger a second time, and he snorted at my absence of a gambler's spirit.

OK, I asked him stoutly, if sunlight did hinder a fire, why did it do it?, and he squinted vaguely and said that it was the superior heat of the sun took away the lesser heat of the piddling coal fire. To me this sounded like the lore of primitive tribes, and I genially told him as much, and looking back it took him quite some affronted time to get the joke. I didn't know at this stage he was going to leave me a fortune and a house, or I might have eagerly concurred with his North East Uplands take on thermophysics.

That was nothing to his theory that he could tell apart the adherents of the numerous Christian denominations by the shape of their eyes. A non-observing agnostic, and completely tolerant towards all faiths, as indeed who wouldn't be stuck up the end of a lonely farm track, Harrison said that spotting an R.C. in the street was simplicity itself. Their eye lines had a particular and subtle and indeed handsome inclination that he had never once failed to detect. Likewise he could spot Methodists by a kind of ever-so-minute pinchedness around the lids, and could distinguish the Wesleyans from the Primitives by the precise degree of that pinchedness. United Reformed, Evangelicals, Free Church of Scotland, Church of Scotland, Congregational, it was all there and highly visible in their eyes. I guffawed, slapped my knee, and said how do you tell a Jehovah's Witness then, Harrison, by their eyes, or by the way they thump on your door and stand there witnessing until you ask them to go away? Harrison turned deadly earnest at that point, and said he had all the time in the world for those folk. They were the only casual as opposed to expected visitors the old widower ever got. No one else would risk driving up a long farm road if they had no idea whether the farmer was in or not. Not so the Witnesses. Harrison was the only person I ever met who actually invited them inside and offered them cake and coffee, and talked at such length about matters in general that some of them almost forgot to do their witnessing.

Further instalment of *Galluses Galore*

Fenton Baggrow aka Jackson Holiday was explaining to the premier and his four security men who the extraordinary strangers facing them were. True enough, no point pretending that they were mega-market garden employees. Anyone could see that at a cursory glance. For a start, if they had been ordinary horticultural technicians they would have been wearing overalls or brown coats, and they weren't. If they had been the wondrously smart suit and tie and braces variety, as described by JH in his letter, that too would have been blindingly obvious. But no they were not.

Instead they looked like a spectacular fashion show. The five strangers, all in their twenties and thirties, comprised four rugged whiskery males (*aw wit greet byurts an varra manly tashes*) and one whisker-free female. The four men wore bright and chromatic sleeved tunics, respectively purple, green, blue and yellow, and beneath these tunics on two of them were linen shirts. Thus Holiday in his smart linen jacket and those two had one thing in sartorial common. The men all wore leather shoes and leather belts and from these belts they had dangling decorated swords and ornate knives, a sight which struck Thomas Purley rather forcefully. To be honest he didn't know whether it was the sight of belts or the sight of weapons that disturbed him most, but frankly he didn't warm to either. The handsome young woman had a pleated blue dress again made of linen and over it was a cloth held up by shoulder straps, the mass of it secured around her body under the arms. The shoulder straps were fastened with a pair of fetching little amber brooches and her dress was edged with some attractive dark blue braid (*reely luffly emprudery weel up till t'varra ightest rooral WI standuds*).

'Who the heck are they?' repeated Thomas Purley. 'And why on earth do my limbs keep refusing to move?'

'I would say severe nervous shock (*a turrible thing is a turrible flait*) is the answer to the second question. I had the same reaction when I first met them. It wore off after about an hour in my case and I could move about as normal.'

. 'An hour? Good. Well I can bear that, but–'

'I have this hunch in your case it might be rather more. Say three or four hours. Or maybe a great deal longer (*strickly spikkin, it cud be mebbe an ear er mare*).'

The premier was getting very angry (*t'top gadger wuss in yan, let's fyass it*). 'We have to be in a bloody Carlisle sausage factory before teatime! Will you tell me who on earth these people are?'

'They're my ancestors.'

'Eh? Rubbish! Why, they're all at least ten years younger than you. Nor do they look remotely like you. They're all more or less good looking, while you're . . .'

'I don't mean my literal ancestors. I mean my ancestors in general. The ones who peopled this general area ever so many moons ago.'

'Bah,' snorted Purley, and his security men also smiled disdainfully (*t'top gadger's boddygad gadgers niffer spokk a bite, but their grinnin fyasses sed it aw*).

Baggrow said politely, 'Let me introduce you to Ulf, Alf, Ralf, Wilf and Gudrun. This one is Ulf (*in t'posh pupple linnen clarse*), this is Alf (*spottin t'cobbled blue hattire*), here's Ralf (*a varra plush canerry yeller*) and last but not least among the men (*in a gey fetshin bottle grin*) is Wilf. This beautiful young woman is Gudrun.'

He then turned to the strangers and addressed them once again in that unique Mandarin Bulgarian Slovakian that had the premier puckering his face incredulously. After a pause, the one called Ulf answered Baggrow in a patient, not unmusical way in the same tongue.

Purley asked, 'What language is that you're speaking (*Pullet sez, wat class ev ootlandish bliddy twang is yon*)?'

165

'Old Cumbrian Norse.'

'Come again.'

'Or Old Norse Cumbrian. It depends which side you're coming from.'

'I've never heard of that one. My guess is they're Bulgarians you're employing here as cheap not to say illegal labour. You think perhaps because you're up in far-flung Cumbria no one can see what you're up to, but I for one can see what's going on. Why the hell you choose to dress them up in *Lord of the Rings* panto is another matter. But that too I expect is technically illegal. There's an old parliamentary paper somewhere on how to treat East Europeans in a reasonably appropriate spirit though it wasn't very popular at the time (*neah point in spoilin them fer when they gah back till Bullgarea, asser*) . . .'

'Old Cumbrian Norse or Old Norse Cumbrian could also be called proto-Old Cumbrian. But it could also be called something a damn sight more musical to the ear.'

'What is that?'

'*Viking!*'

At that, both the premier and his security men seemed to feel their immobility was definitely scheduled for at least another four or five hours.

'Ulf, Alf, Ralf, Wilf and Gudrun are all Vikings. They all speak Viking also known as Old Cumbrian Norse or Old Norse Cumbrian or proto-Old Cumbrian. As it happens that's just sufficiently like the dialect at the far end of Bew-castle crossed with the dialect at the far end of Roadhead, crossed with the twang at the far end of Kershopefoot crossed with the way they talk at the far end of Bailey . . .'

'Yes?'

'For me to have no trouble with it. It's a bit like talking to your very old grandad who's talking about his earliest memories of his own crusty grandpa back in the 1890s who just happens to be reminiscing about his hoary old grandaddy of the 1840s . . . and so on back about twenty generations, till you get to Ulf, a Viking chieftain, and these four splendid subjects of his.'

'I don't believe you for a minute. But just for the moment assuming it's true, this Ulf who I still maintain is one of your illegal Bulgarian strawberry pickers, you say he is a sort of local premier, a sort of very important leader (*a varra top gadger*)?'

'Exactly. He's a warrior chieftain settled in this part of the Pennines. Gudrun here is his younger sister. Alf, Ralf and Wilf are Ulf's loyal and trustworthy tribute chieftains, all of them brave and fearless, even reckless warriors. Gudrun you might be interested to know is half promised to Ralf as his wife, providing and as long as he promises to keep up his martial prowess.'

'Aha. Mm. Let's assume I go along with this preposterous rigmarole for the time being. I know you and they are speaking a bona fide language alright, which again I maintain is Bulgarian. But just accepting for the moment that it is Old Lancashire Norse . . .'

'Old Cumbrian Norse (*Owd Cummerlan Norse*).'

'Old Cumbrian Norse or Hoary Viking or proto-thingummy. The point is I'm a very busy man and I've never had the leisure to mug any of it up with the Linguaphone CDs. I neither speak nor understand it, so I need you Jackson Holiday as my Bulgarian/Viking two-way translator. You are required to be the conduit, the go-between, the operator, the enabler, the facilitator, the coach, the . . . etc. As you know I'm used to having my most casual words translated all over the world, from Strasbourg to Washington to Tel Aviv to Doncaster, and now here is your golden chance to redeem yourself after this appalling act of wilful deception you've perpetrated.'

It was at this stage that Ulf obviously became painfully curious about the man in the wellies and his four burly minders, all of them unable to move a muscle other than the organ of speech. Baggrow told him in Old Cumbrian

Norse that no, the oldish man in the shiny black footwear was not a local chieftain leader but the chieftain leader of the whole of a nation, this vast nation of which this local fiefdom was but a minor part. Ulf for his part looked a trifle incredulous though he made no pejorative demur. Baggrow throughout the one-act drama that follows acted as zealous two-way translator, informing Purley what the Vikings were saying and also keeping the Vikings up to date by conscientiously running past them anything the Great Chieftain in the Wellingtons had to say.

ULF: This Great Chieftain. Can you describe to us his principal deeds of valour?

BAGGROW: (after honest thought) (*pezzlin his brains fer inspirashun fer a minnit er mare*) He does not do mighty deeds in the usually accepted mighty deed-doing sense. He makes many mighty laws instead. Then other willing vassals enact these laws.

ALF: Relate to us these mighty laws enacted by the Great Chieftain.

THOMAS PURLEY: And don't you make a pig's ear of it, Holiday! Be accurate and truthful in so far as you are able to create no offence (*diven't thee oppen thi daft mooth an let thi bliddy brens faw oot*).

BAGGROW: The most important law in this local fiefdom where we currently dally, is the Strict Prohibition of the Belt.

THOMAS PURLEY: (extremely aghast) (*flait even mare stiff*) Ugh. I mean gah. I mean agh. I mean shut–

RALF: (*adjustin iss bonny ledder belt wit t'owd chool encrustit dagger as big as a gulley knife hingin frae it*) You are saying that this nobleman in the shining black high-sided slippers will punish those who wear belts? Is there just and proper cause for this?

BAGGROW: Ahem. Only in this one fiefdom and among the grown males does he enact it. He believes that the wearing of a belt as an engirdlement-means, is a sign of sloth, rebellion, disrespect for one's grey-bearded elders (*impidence ter owd fwoak wise in ears is the bliddy least ev it*) and worse.

PURLEY: Gah. Tone it down! For God's sake tone it down! Remember who you're talking to. Tailor your talk according to your perceived audience. Make it a whole lot less gratuitously explosive if you please.

BAGGROW: The Lord of the Lofty Sided Black Slippers enacts that in this remote hilly fiefdom grown males may not wear belts, nor may they optionally wear nothing at all for their girdling. Instead they must always sport the Flying Bifurcated Thongs with Firmly Anchoring Buttons. Yes, sir, you see these ones I am wearing? I must wear these for this strong-minded lord who rules the whole of this land, not just our local fiefdom. Else will I haply face a sizeable fine (*nut ezactly danegeld but summat varra simla*). Worse, if I rebel and adhere to the proscribed belt, and keep on thus perniciously adhering, I must also face a dismal dungeon spell.

PURLEY: Gah, Holiday! Do you have to be so appallingly bald in putting it all so appallingly baldly? Do you have to be so relentlessly – what's the word? Something to do with Vera. Honest? No. Veracious? Some quintessentially unreliable variable in any case. Can't you hedge man, did no one ever teach you how to hedge (*wat's wrang wit lakin aw milly-mootht if it kips things tickin alang, asser*)? You're supposed to be a market gardener after all. Can't you drag your heels a bit more and put in a few provisos such as 'it can be envisaged' 'in a sense' and 'up to a point'?

BAGGROW: It can be envisaged, sir, that the local men did not like such a capricious enactment. Worse still the Flying Bifurcated Thongs must be ever visible to the watching world on pain of substantial fine or thwarting dungeon. Thus on a cold day if a jerkin or over-tunic (*owd-feshiont keitel er ower-tyeunick*) should hide the same Thongs, the local male must tie the thong loop twain about his hapless ears so that they be ever conspicuous to the watching world.

WILF: What? About his *ears* did you say?

RALF: About his hapless *ears*?

ULF: About the local male's two *ears*?

GUDRUN: About the poor man's wretched *ears*? For shame surely!

PURLEY: Shame alright! Gross distortion is only the half of it. I blame this damn word for word translation instead of a spirited free rendering. An appalling job you're doing, Holiday, with that Dog Latin of yours or Hound Trail Cumbrian or whatever it is. There really was no cause whatever for you to tell them about the Ear Suspension Option. You could have kept that back as sensitive, highly confidential and altogether by the by, in any competent and proper free translation.

And so it went. The Vikings now looked with pained and open hostility at this strange and seemingly cruel elderly chieftain (*in 2018 Tommy Pullet wuss sisty-eight an even in*

170

his own patty sum sed he wuss clingin on till t'addictif trap-pins ev poor) in his glaring black high-sided slippers only recently purchased by Holiday from the West Cumberland Farmers. It was evident to Ulf, Alf, Ralf, Wilf and Gudrun that this old chieftain made his local vassals and serfs humiliated at their most vulnerable level, i.e. the visible means of what engirdled their sensitive and hidden parts. It was an item of apparel which as well as being decorative and highly-functional ought to have been warrior-manly, but instead he forced on them this disgraceful dunce and jester apparel. They pressed Baggrow for further examples of the High Black Slippered Lord's law-making in the generous hope that they might just find something in his favour. Baggrow scratched his chin and instanced the compulsory Five Pieces of Fresh Fruit and Vegetables Law enacted two years ago. Since then the whole of the overlord's subjects, from here to London via Kidderminster and everywhere to the right and left, were obliged to show the overlord's numerous roving clerks, official receipts from the markets and stalls where they had purchased their fruits and vegetables. These officials invariably wore orange jerkins and caps with hard and elliptical peaks, and they checked that the obligatory fruit and vegetables had all been itemised and receipted. Should the subjects have failed to keep the receipts or otherwise be unable to prove their purchases, they would face a hefty fine and in persistent cases a salutary dungeon spell.

'Which leads us,' said Baggrow, 'to the new Fatness Laws. These have already been mulled over by this Black Slippered Overlord's Two-Tier Witanagemot (*ee meant t'Hussies ev Come Ins and t' Hussies ev Lurds*) down in his far away capital, and it seems as if they will soon be enacted everywhere as law.'

Gudrun smiled her relief and said, 'Very pleased I am to hear that. That a portly warrior and a thick-thighed maid and a lardy matron will be justly rewarded for a bouncing girth. I myself am a slim, starved pigeon with no stout shanks or robust arms, and more blushing shame for me.'

'At last!' Alf concurred. 'At last this overlord shows some manly guile and foxlike strategy. This fruit and vegetable law he surely does as a jest, the kind a shrunken old crone not a virile overlord would enact. Surely all that pimp-and-jackass's fruit guzzling will make every man and woman subject skite and skitter until their teeth fair rattle. As for all those ass-feed turnips, carrots and the like, they will cause them to fart and fizz like so many snorting old she-goats. It is good to hear that he has dropped his playful jesting and will now reward the broad-girthed and the truly enormous for their stirring bulk and manly embonpoints.'

Baggrow hesitated as he saw Purley's eye-language urging him to change the subject (*Tommy Pullet wuss squintin an gurnin like buggery, tryin ter git Baggra ter chunter on aboot tomorra's wedder er sek like*). Then he blurted: 'I'm sorry, I'm afraid it is the opposite case. This high-booted shiny-shod all powerful overlord does not love his fat subjects, and he thinks they should be punished.'

There was a general gasping from the Vikings, and Gudrun cried, 'For shame!' once again. Then Ulf, Alf, Ralf and Wilf slowly advanced as one warrior towards the still frozen premier, whereupon the latter cried out in great alarm to Baggrow: 'Bloody hell! Your damn word for word translation once again! They're turning ugly Holiday, can't you see? I believed you when you told me no one would harm us, and this is where my credulity leads me. Look, I think you need to do a bit of emergency PR at this point. I think you need to whatsit. Reframe. Recast. Change tack. Say white is black, or green or red for that matter. I want you to stop them in their tracks right away. Tell them, will you please, that I want to do some crisis management consultation and to run something past them (*Pullet sez, lookster, ah want them ter hod their bliddy hossis so's ah can lait summat past em in t'contempry manazherial sense*).'

'Run something past them? Are you sure?'

'Yes and once I've run it past them they'll see how I know to keep all parties happy by all possible pragmatic means (*sister, ah's a voorsatile marraboy fer aw sissons, er my nyam's nut Tommy Pullet*).'

End of instalment of *Galluses Galore*

10

I have been remiss in glossing over the manner of the ending of the affair between my wife and Garnett. This is partly because like everyone else I skirt the most painful things in life but also because the very act of mentioning what is disturbing seems to give it a pernicious continuance and a life of its own. But the other and arguably pardonable excuse is the merciless and demoralising way it had all unravelled before my wife's disbelieving eyes.

Liz was never to tell Garnett about her first transcendent experience in that village-hall venue, the vision of something beautiful and infinite and indestructible. The musician Reverend Wiley with theatrical indifference had tried to tear up enduring scripture as if it were disposable confetti, and she had been the beneficiary of his vain attempt. Nor did she ever tell her lover about her second village-hall vision, where the focus of another possible spiritual transformation was no less than Garnett himself. She alluded to it obliquely and in the end almost embarrassed, and certainly unintelligibly as far as Garnett was concerned.

'You seem always,' she told him bravely matter of fact, a few weeks before their parting, 'to be so infinitely self-contained.'

Her inflection was rueful rather than critical and he acknowledged as much. He glanced at her shrewdly after first leaning back from staring at a very long explanatory caption. They were down in Manchester looking around an art gallery while her story to me was she was on a shopping spree with Garnett's sister Jane. He said: 'Really? What makes you say that I wonder? Are you sure?'

'Yes,' she said with the calm if poignant certainty of her seven decades. 'Yes I am extremely sure. I have seen it in all its intensity.'

Garnett raised his eyes in muted irony. He had been divorced twice and had a total of five children aged between fifteen and thirty-five, none of them living with him, though they all frequently visited his North Cumbrian hideaway.

'I think you might have seen something else,' he said. 'Apart from any other consideration, I'm not particularly intense.'

She gave a flinch of agreement and after a while said, 'Yes indeed. You're quite right. Maybe that's not the word I mean. So what's the implication of that I wonder. Joe Gladstone you know is extraordinarily intense. You would agree immediately if you were to meet him. You could say he's a by-word for it, the living personification.'

This might well have been construed as an elliptical attempt to needle him with jealousy. But he showed no signs of being ruffled, nor had she intended it that way. Nevertheless his calm and unaffected smile at the mention of me, the aged irascible third party, seemed to offer further proof of an unshakeable serenity.

They moved to the gallery coffee bar where Liz glanced about her, lowered her voice and said: 'Once or twice I've seen it in your eyes, Patrick. It was always painfully hypnotic and I couldn't stop looking at it. This extraordinary expression which seems to come from your very depths. It's as if there you are safe and protected no matter what the external circumstances are. And the corollary of that is that at bottom, at very bottom, you don't really need anyone, do you? You've survived two divorces, you live in a beautiful but lonely, far-flung place, and yet you seem wholly incapable of loneliness.'

He smiled and touched her hand at this point and gave it a squeeze which she subsequently told me was remarkable for its profound and uncanny absence of reassurance.

There was more or less nothing there in that squeeze other than the muscular sensation of his fingers. Stunned by that touch that wasn't a touch but a wounding mirage of one, she suddenly saw herself reflected in the mirror behind the café counter. White-haired and lined despite all the careful make-up, she had looked she told me, like Garnett's much older sister and at a stretch could have been his erstwhile teenage mother. In a split second, and to turn the knife in the wound, she beheld what all people see when they embark on an adulterous affair: that there is no end to its inconclusive and unresolvable nature, no light at the end of the tunnel as such, unless the whole hog is to be embraced, viz. confession, ructions, hell on earth, divorce and start again. Otherwise it is to be an endless itinerary of subterfuge and lying and a temporary, tormenting and partial account of each other for evermore.

More to the point, and notwithstanding the reformed cultural guidelines of 2008, she was unarguably an old woman, even if she had her looks and most of her wits about her. What then was the likely and credible flavour of her future, given that any kind of future after three score and ten is a welcome bonus rather than a cast-iron certainty? That amnesic touch of his was mute acknowledgement of that choice irony. He must on some level be reflecting that in seven years time his lover would be eighty, and frankly no one, not a single soul, not even in satire or surreal cinema, is having affairs at eighty years old. He on the other hand in 2015 would be only seventy but guaranteed to be looking sixty or even an attractive adolescent of fifty-five at a pinch.

It wasn't as simple as her seeing the end writ large at that particular point in time. But like a disquieting physical symptom, that naïve act of hand-holding had given her some indication of the crisis to come. The body finds it difficult and troublesome to lie, whereas the mouth can embroider and dissimulate for evermore. For the rest of the afternoon they went round the gallery conscientiously discussing everything, sometimes in accord and sometimes not when it came to graphic skill and the spirit of the artist who had created this reassuringly solid and finite object of their attention. Liz at one stage was convinced that Patrick liked the more subtly self-regarding, cooler, even arctic of the practitioners, then doubted that suspicion and chastised herself for it, then had it reaffirmed, then decided she would blank out these cascading and debilitating nuances of doubt. She would discount her appreciation of his appreciation of the various pictures, on the grounds that another person's taste in art is surely not necessarily indicative of deep emotional affiliation and sensitive sympathy towards oneself.

Or is it? At any rate the affair found its natural limits as Garnett's warmth or Liz's perception of such warmth faltered, and which Liz understood as his gradual awakening to her age and her mortality. Just possibly he glimpsed her on a day, a morning or an evening, where instead of looking hearteningly young for her age as he always did, she looked heartlessly old for her age. Possibly he scented the wrinkled vulnerable octogenarian on the horizon and he selfishly shuddered. Possibly he asked himself why he had encouraged this strange and eccentric business in the first place. As the permutations of cooling and steadying and settling and stagnating began to happen . . . Liz was also confronted with the confusing similarities of her two disorienting visions. It seemed as if she had conflated the two, inasmuch as the indestructibility of that which was venerable and sacred had seemed to be mirrored there in some parallel way in her glimpse of Patrick's tender and invulnerable soul.

I told her in that week of confession it could have been several things. Possibly that image of Garnett corresponded to his purest self, a discrete part which was there only for his children or in his private communion with himself.

Meaning it was just a fleeting part of the man rather than the whole of him. Or could it even be a kind of projection of herself onto the focus of her attention, her own simplest and purest self projected onto what she had seen under that transfixing red light in the quaint and resonant dance hall?

She looked at me with pain in her eyes. 'I saw him as good, and he wasn't. He wasn't bad, but he wasn't good either. And if I was just seeing myself heightened and exalted in his eyes I wasn't seeing anything good there either.'

'How do you know you are not a good person?' I asked. 'You are better than most folk I know.'

'But I have been unfaithful. And I was very old when I decided to be unfaithful and there's no excuse for that.'

'We are all allowed to err. Anyway age has damn all to do with it, has it?'

'I am really very confused when you argue on my behalf. You are calm and dispassionate now but tomorrow you'll be ranting at me for what I did instead of forgiving me. I don't blame you for doing that but–'

'I know. But we are all allowed to err. Me included.'

'Poor old Joe,' she said.

'Bollocks to poor old Joe,' I sniffed. 'I don't mind being bloody old Joe or even nasty old Joe but not poor old Joe.'

Further instalment of *Galluses Galore*

The very anxious premier (*t'varra flait top gadger*) had been begging Fenton Baggrow, who he believed was a market-garden magnate called Jackson Holiday, to intercede on his behalf with the angry Vikings. So far he had breathlessly assured Ulf, Alf etc. that his Obligatory Braces Act was only a piece of experimental pilot legislation, that he was only testing the water (*juss yah fyeut powkt in t'watter*), only running it past the Cumbrians, that he needed really to touch base with them at this point to see how the land lay, and that nothing was carved in stone. This welter of pilot, water, running, base and stone metaphors even in Baggrow's nuanced and effortful Old Cumbrian Norse version (*Owd Cummerlan Norse fer expurt linwistick conniesirs*) made the Vikings both perplexed and irritated. This man who had been frozen in all his limbs, wasn't talking their kind of metaphors of eagles, crags, suns, hinds, does, hounds etc. Instead he was using odd comparisons which offered no picture, because none of the Vikings could see the water or the stone or the running or the base that he was talking about. At bottom, Ulf told Baggrow, what they all disliked about Purley was that he didn't act like a virile flesh and blood man but like some sort of banquet-hall jester whose jests weren't remotely funny (*ee wuss like a cloon wat liked lakin aboot, but frankly iss lakin wussn't a hunnert psent entertainin*). To put it another way, Gudrun said, he talked a kind of ghost language where the comparisons and flights of fancy had no picture, meaning no poetry, hence no life about them. And he was supposed to be the chief leader of the whole land as well as the foremost chieftain of this remote and hilly province, was he?

Wilf said: 'Making one's subjects look idiots by wearing flying birfurcated thong loops around their ears, that is very hard to forgive.'

Baggrow remarked to Purley, 'What they don't understand, these Vikings, is that you manage to rule the country by behaving like a school prefect (*juss like a bussy owd grammer schyeul prefeck*). It is a type of rule unknown and inimical to them for more than one reason (*cos it's doon-reet forren ter their natral ways*).'

'Quite right,' said Purley, quaintly gratified, as if that very stable old-fashioned English word 'prefect' had blanked out all this hideous martial warrior stuff. 'I was Head of House fifty years ago back in 1968. I ruled with a firm and often fair rod and I received more than one commendation from those who understood my unique style (*ah wuss defnitly weel liked by them wat weel liked us*).'

Baggrow sighed and said they didn't have school prefects in Viking society, neither in the old days nor the transposed nowadays. Hence Premier Purley's attitude profoundly puzzled them when it was understood as his chosen means of ruling a whole country, or even a minor province such as Cumbria.

'This school prefect attitude,' Baggrow continued sternly, 'this form monitor (*foam monnity*) approach, this backdoor control (*backdooer er nowt, asser*) by the school sneak? It is just bare-faced bullying by another name, in my considered opinion. There's also a posh adjective that sits next to it very comfortably (*a fancy laal tecknicle tum wat fits it like a gluff*).'

Purley tried to furrow his brow but it too was immobilised unfortunately (*Pullet tried ter gurn an gripe up his fyass but it wuss as frozz as a petrifit highcicle*). He asked, 'Pragmatic? Creatively and Adaptively Self-Protective?'

'No. The word is unctuous. It means oily. The oil runs everywhere (*t'wuld's it's slipry hoyster*). It even runs in places you wouldn't expect, in foreign countries that specialise in oil. Back here in Britain one day it's braces, and you must wear them, because the school prefect thinks it keeps things in good old-fashioned order, whereas flashy belts are too much like sloppy anarchy. The next day it's issue them with a punitive fine, because they're persistently and flagrantly fat. Then make them pay for their operations (*in t'schyeul sannytoryham sick bay*) because they're obese, and this school prefect who knows that the fat kids, especially the fat and powerless juniors, are damn good scapegoats, he thinks it's a damn good idea that will win all the lesser bullies to our side (*diffide an ryeul is oor schyeul ryeul*). Then people who break the school rules and have the anti-social gall (*aunty soshul gull*) to produce fully grown children inside the school in flagrant anti-social circumstances, these single parents who hang about discrediting the school . . . the school sneak will draw the school's attention to them. And if they are disabled single parents hanging about and discrediting the same school, even more is their culpable shame when hauled before the tutting prefect in their wheelchairs . . . (*noo than, noo than, noo than, thoo's nut spost ter be lakin aboot makkin laal babbies in a willchur at oor hexpense, asser!*)

'Why stop with the prefect's school though (*why hod thisel back wen thoo can let flee in proper style*)? There are schools all over the world after all. First you bully them in your own fair land, then you take the next sensible step and bully them abroad. You take over their school, and show them how to run it even if it means bloodying a lot of noses when they don't recognise and don't want English school rules. You get your transatlantic school governor pal on your side and your one or two pragmatic governor friends in Europe (*neah kwestuns asst as lang as ivvrythin targes alang nicely*). You spread your unctuous oil where they have their own kind of oil that you need from them a damn sight more than they need your slippery elm kind. You take over all their foreign schools to get at it, and tell them you are going to make this a free and fair school of a type wholly unknown to them (*frank, filless and free juss like t' guid owd Peeple noospyaper*).

'Even though you are seen to be a school bully and a school sneak you will bring freeness and fairness, that is what has had us all stunned across the years, across all the generations and the Nordic races, including Old Vikings and New Cumbrians, Premier Purley. This is what Ulf, Alf, Ralf, Wilf and Gudrun see as not a mite paradoxical and ironical and blackly humorous and so on and so forth . . .'

You might have noticed that the premier (*t'top gadger*) had very little to say as Baggrow delivered this torrent of tendentious and attitudinising polemic (*poppygander, pattysan pollymick, an wuss*) with all these childish metaphors of bullies, schools, sneaks, and monitors. Unfortunately for Baggrow, the comparisons and the images were too homely, too school story in a school annual by a crackling fireside with toasted pikelets (*tyasty laal crumpits frae t'schyeul tukksop*) and the intended wounds inevitably went only skin deep into Thomas Purley. Nevertheless the premier (*t'top gadger*) could not help but be moved to sudden speech.

'Holiday,' he said rather excitedly. 'There's something I have to say to you.'

'Yes?'

'You're not a market gardener! Do you realise that? Never in the memory of man (*nivver awivver awoor*)! I don't know what your trade is other than rouser of rabbles, some of them Old Cumbrian Norsefolk, but it's definitely not a market-garden magnate. No gardener worth his salt would come out with all that incontinent propaganda guff when he could be profitably employed pruning his perennials or mulching his mimosa or dusting down his last year's grobags.'

'Whatever my profession,' said Baggrow sharply, 'you have a very serious problem on your hands, I think.'

Purley looked at him with patronage. 'I doubt it. I've told you to tell them in your best Old Westmorland Norse that I'm ever adaptable and ready to water down some of the compulsory braces stuff. Furthermore perhaps I won't after all jail people over fourteen stones in this present parliamentary period. There is always room for elasticity, or I wouldn't be a successful politician but a contemptible novice always tripping over his own careless words (*allus cowpin heedlang ower iss own daft woods*).'

Baggrow approached his country's leader as if to impart a confidence. He said in a low, very calm voice. 'Because I'm your two-way translator, you are even more in my hands than in theirs! So far in my translation, I'm sorry to say, I have been regularly putting a "will most certainly not" in front of every "change his mind". I have also been negativing all your promised change of heart, all your free and fair and adaptable approach. They now think you are even more sternly unbending than the admiring tabloids do. You know, the ones where your forthright words are squeezed comfortably between the breasts and backsides on page three (*t'top gadger promises sturn akshun! stuck nicely atween Tina's nyakt cliffage an Mimi's bare behint*). To be honest, Ulf here is getting very impatient to give you a vigorous piece of his mind, and I'm more or less having to hold him off.'

The premier shuddered as violently as his petrifaction permitted. 'You bas– You. What did I ever do to you (*wat did ah ivver dyeuh till sek as thee, thoo bas–*)?'

'You tried to make me loop braces round my lugholes, when I didn't even want them round my tits in the first place! I'm a belt man, and always have been and always will be, and I'm not the only one in this good old-fashioned land of ours! Worse than that, you're itching to do things like jail Tunstall's Cousin Aggie for being fat! As if being old and fat and living in Haltwhistle, in the exact geographical centre of Britain isn't a big enough load for any one individual to bear in 2018!'

Purley temporised (*owd Pullet ed ed raither mare than enuf bi noo ev feytin an fratchin issel*). 'OK, hard man. What is it you want?'

'A signed and dated retraction of the Braces Act! A signed and dated retraction of the Obesity Laws! I've got them both conveniently typed out here in my pocket, so all you need to do is sign them.'

Purley fumed as best he could in his frozen state. 'But I can't move a muscle, never mind wield a pen.'

'I'll soon cure that. It's only the nervous shock that's paralysed you. I'll just tell my friends to go back inside that gate and once they've disappeared you'll get all your movement back. You'll soon be repealing legislation as fast as the best of them.'

The premier looked as sullen as a peevish child (*t'top gadger wuss sulkin like a bairn wid a puzzent fyass*). 'And what if I–?'

'If you renege on our agreement, or try to have me arrested by these security men, or go public about me and my Old Norse friends with the TV men and the journalists down there . . .'

'Yes?'

'I will send my Vikings round to see you! Ulf, Alf, Ralf and Wilf will go vengeful walkabout (*Ulf, Alf, Ralf an Wilf will git theirsels doon ter Lunnon an then thoo'll bliddy weel know wat's wat*)! Wherever you are and however you are! Even from my jail cell I will let them know by unique, extrasensory means my wounded feelings at your treachery. They won't need a bus pass or a diesel runabout ticket or a longboat (*fleein like t'wind doon aw t'canals an watterwez*) to get themselves from Carlisle to London to see you. They have ways and they have means! They don't actually walk through walls like so many common or market-garden illusionists, but they have a blasé way with one or two of the dimensions.'

'Which dimensions?'

'Oh, Time. Ah, Space. Can't remember the others, but that needn't concern you. I would very rapidly agree to my demands if I were you. In the meantime, while you're thinking it over, Gudrun, whose warrior father got about a bit and surveyed many hoary lands from his wave-breasting longboat, has some meaty sayings (*mitty laal woods an profurbs*) from the Old Icelandic for you. Her dad brought her back some books from ancient Iceland, not just the justly famous sagas and the equally note-worthy eddas, but a kind of fireside wisdom book. It was written by a wise-beyond-her-years Reykjavik maiden called Solrun. It has, Gudrun tells me, one or two pithy maxims relating to body weight, to which you might profitably hearken.'

There was a strange and protracted pause before the premier came out with an unexpected accusation.

'An actor!' he cried in a loud acknowledging voice (*a bliddy damn akter! gollers Tommy Pullet*). 'That's what you are! I've just twigged. 'Market Garden Magnate' is just a crafty acronym to mask your identity. MGM. Acting is the name of your game. You're a walking cryptic crossword (*like a bliddy owd hacrustic er a crosswood er sundry udder mindstritchin tizzers*) or my name's not Thomas Purley (*er ah's Max Biegriff, nut Tommy Pullet*).'

Gudrun approached the premier and waggled her pretty finger admonitorily (*she shakks er bonny but stoorn laal mitt in iss freetened fyass*). 'Hearken, Lord of the High Sided and Why Beat about the Bush Quite Ungainly Black Slippers (*betwin me an thee, thi shiny wellies is a doonreet emparrassment wedder thoo's a lowcal chifftun er a varra top gadger frae t'Hussies ev Pallyment*).'

It was a testament to Purley's mental alertness in these most trying conditions that he became suddenly and thoroughly incensed. 'That last bit's your lying embellishment, Holiday! Why, this young Old Norsewoman has never even heard of the Houses of Parliament, so how could she have come out with that?'

Gudrun continued deafly. 'Your cruel persecution of the stout and huge-girthed deserves the just censure of all decent folk! Listen to this Norse translation of Solrun's Wise Young Woman's Old Icelandic Pillow Book. Take heed of what she has to say about the virtues of a cultivated fatness and the unarguable personal and social advantages of a deliberate obesity . . .'

Gudrun declaimed in a tender and expressive Old Norse soprano. 'Adage 3a. "Art possessed of unbelievably outsize thighs? Knowledge's crown jewel be thy prize!" Well? What do you say to that, belt-hating tyrant?'

'Ah–'

'Adage 3b. "When yon maid have a bulging ham, be she assuredly no intellectual sham." Confess, froward man, does that not pierce your obstinate heart?'

'Up to a p–'

'Adage 4a. "A giant backside portends general knowledge encyclopaedically wide." Could that be improved upon in its universal pertinacity?'

'From one point of–'

'Adage 4b. "Thy vastly huge behind walketh in the sunlight of thy insatiably enquiring mind." And yet before me is this man who persecutes such bouncing lardy heroes for their fearless corpulence!'

'Adage 5a. "Look ye, an colossal belly affords any warrior much copious intellectual welly." Tell me again, capricious chief of chieftains, doesn't–?'

'Hang on,' snorted the authoritative Lord of the WCF Wellies himself. 'What sort of pig's arse translation is that? As per all this High Sided Slipper rigmarole they keep throwing at me, we know damn fine they didn't have wellies in Viking or Icelandic days (*neah sek thing, owny gussets an brogs an warrya sandals an aw wat nut*). Even someone like me who doesn't speak Old Lake District Norse knows that simple primary-school fact. More to the point, and allowing for your risible poetic licence, even if they had employed the wellington to stop their feet getting wet in the longboats, they wouldn't use the abbreviated word in a secondary metaphorical sense of impetus or clout or élan (*himpetus er cloot er hillan in t'hogshillary sense*).'

'Granted,' agreed Baggrow. 'Yes, that last adage was a rather free translation I admit. You see welly makes such a nice economical rhyme with belly, I couldn't resist it. Whereas in my rendering of the Old Cumbrian Norse translation of Solrun's Old Icelandic, I actually employed the word they have for gut to rhyme with the term they use for a young warrior's lusty priapic vigour. Anyway, Premier, you try finding a rapid rhyme for calfskin brogue or high-sided shiny black slipper. You're a better impromptu epic bard and maiden's pillow book translator than me if you can.'

Thomas Purley grunted. 'Well I can confirm that the word "rogue" rhymes with "brogue" (*sister, rug rimes wid bliddy brug*)! A word that should never be far from the tip of your scoundrel's tongue, Jackson Holiday the kidnapper! And frankly I've had enough of these pithy sayings from bygone Reykjavik about big hams and stout bellies and outsize maidenly backsides getting you into Old Icelandic MENSA by the back door. I'd much prefer to go down to modern Cumbrian Carlisle and its bloody sausage factory and some species of normality. OK, Holiday, you win. You can tell your Old Viking Norsemen and this finger–pointing Norse-woman to get back inside your property, and I promise you I'll sign your bits of paper. And while we're at it, a modern and scientific citizen I might be, but they do actually look to me like they could walk through walls if need be. At first I thought they were odd-looking actors like you, but no they're altogether something else (*summat else awtergidder an wat it is ah hev neah bliddy noshun*).

End of final instalment of *Galluses Galore*
End of *GALLUSES GALORE*
By Joe Gladstone of Mallstown

Let me by way of finale tell you about the height of mature wisdom as it relates to any age, any generation, any land, any period in history. It was 1966, a year before the junta took over in Greece, and Liz and I and six-year-old Desmond were enjoying a cheap backpacking holiday on Ithaca. The latter as you know is an Ionian island with a certain literary significance, home to the mother and father of all epic love stories which is also a testament to hope, perseverance and the courageous confrontation of cruelty and evil. We went there because in those days it was remote, an awkward hop from then unvisited Kefalonia which also has a certain ubiquitous literary prominence forty years later. We stayed in dirt-cheap, beautiful rooms in the little harbour capital Vathi and went on longish hikes during the day. Because Desmond was only six, and it was often boiling hot, it meant his legs got tired and he opted to ride on his father's broad shoulders.

The thing about six-year-olds is they have no such things as abstract moral principles or abstract ethical rules. We were walking a lovely deserted hill road between Anoghi and Exoghi, the smell of sage ripe in our nostrils, when Desmond, though chirruping and whistling and happy, became momentarily bored. Up there on the howdah of my shoulders, it occurred to him it would be pleasant fun to rattle the comical bald patch on the skull of the beast of burden below. He did so with his small but forceful hand, relished the boiled-egg echo, exploded with merriment, and proceeded to do it again, though with both hands this time and in alternating syncopation. It was such excellent sport as they say in Shakespeare, it was so incredibly funny, that contrapuntal slap on the pater's pate, was it not? For five minutes or so he played a competent diminished rallentando, the boiled-egg sonata by D. Gladstone, the pintsize percussionist. It was one of those experiences that was borderline bearable, inasmuch as his drumming wasn't painful, nor all that irritating, just redolent of something that might never stop this side of eternity because its perpetrator found it so addictively enjoyable. Also, the scorching heat was a factor . . . I was sweating with my restless load while also chuckling appreciatively with Liz and the aerial drummer.

Boredom can either stifle or engender creativity. Desmond tired of the drumming and found that he could easily seize my thirty-year-old's beard and yank it playfully

188

rather than painfully. As rapid and lateral elaboration, he could also seize the long hair at the sides of my head and proceed to make interesting nautical knots in the foliage. Once the hair knotting had palled, he put his hands over my eyes as we struggled up the hill road, so that the mule with the cross-knitted thatch would perforce stumble as it guessed where it was walking rather than confidently negotiate the path. Throughout, the comedian up above roared hugely at his own genius, his innocent and entertaining hooliganism. I meanwhile kept tight hold of my precious charge, and Liz had him supported at both sides so that the restless tormentor could not come to any possible grief. My young wife was having galeforce hysterics at this sage-scented spectacle of course . . .

Four years on it was 1970, and Desmond was ten years old. It was a cold winter's evening and exhausted from working all day on a new cookery book, I was snoozing deeply in the armchair. Again Desmond felt bored, but as ever was productively inspired. Where other kids might have drawn a black spider on my now much larger bald patch, Desmond had larger ambitions. He vanished to find a couple of sheets of my typing paper as well as a roll of sellotape. He ripped the paper into a dozen little bits and inscribed something very important with a biro on each. Then monitoring my Rip van Winkle snoring, he got feverishly busy with the sellotape before producing something relevant to operations from his toy cupboard.

I awoke with a start to a moderate but significant blow to the chest. As always when I wake from deep slumber, I had no idea where I was or who I was or why the hell I was. I was only thirty-five, but it could have been an early heart attack and I squawked hysterically in my alarm.

I took in a hallucinatory scene. Desmond was stood there in front of me with a poised rubber ball in his hand. I was looking at him via decorative tent flaps of a sort, or rather small paper pelmets. Two of these were affixed

189

symmetrically to my temples by ragged strips of sellotape. There was also a square of paper stuck on my nose end, which meant I was squinting hard to focus through the ambient foliage. I looked down and there was another bit of paper taped to the centre of my stomach. In biro in a ten-year-old's scrawl a number was written. It was 100.

The ball came flying and whanged me with force on the tip of my nose. Desmond hooted loudly and boomed a victorious number. The number he roared was 50. To defer more aeronautic sallies I stood up and walked across to the mirror above the sideboard. I stooped and saw a man in his bleary middle thirties with a dozen small paper targets pinned to his person, a living Aunt Sally. My belly was the bull's eye at 100. Each temple was 25. The nose was 50. The chin was also 50. Each pectoral weighed in at 75. In terms of anatomical hierarchy his system was erratic but original and his own. Still brainless with sleep, I grunted and returned to sprawling in my favourite chair. He immediately resumed his torrential potshotting and over the next ten minutes achieved a personal best of 275.

To get back to the height of mature wisdom, it is just possibly this. The comic spirit as enacted in the spirit of a hilarious child is surely the prime indicator here. It is hilarious but innocent, delightfully insane but delightfully harmless, excessive in its bounty and its inspired superfluity. It spurns the corruptions of violence, cruelty, pride, avarice, ambition as they get in the way of pure inconsequential fun. On the spur of the moment, it gives of its comic excess and has no time to plot and coordinate and fret the dreary old passage of future years.

There is an enduring connection between that and Liz's extraordinary experiences in the raucous dance hall, though I am not sure what it is. But this idea of bountiful giving is always there at the root of these important things . . .

* * *

There was a shortlist for the dialect competition but it was only revealed on the night of the presentation itself, which took place inside Carlisle's vast market hall. Then followed some leisurely retrospective analysis as the chairman tutted and bemoaned the tragic onerousness of such an impossible task. There were six on the shortlist, hence five of them learnt at mesmerising length how they had been seriously in the running for the enormous prize but in the end got nothing apart from an honourable mention. I was not on the shortlist, much less the one who was able to give Liz her fifty thousand pounds apology. I sat there infinitely stunned, as I learnt that all that labour on *Galluses Galore* had not even earned a two-second mention, not even a public disparagement of the quirkiness and/or disgracefulness of my unusual submission. I even wondered whether they had ever received the bloody thing through the post in the first place, as supine and absolute silence was the one thing I had never envisaged after all those weeks of graft and sweat.

They talk about body blows and this was one of them. Short snatches from all six virtuosos were read aloud in the packed hall, each one worse than the last. There was sentimental doggerel about 'sun-cappt Skidda' and 'bonny laal Borrodyal'; there were derivative tales about a duck race being subverted by rogue competitors; another old chestnut variant about a farmer getting drunk at Penrith auction and losing all his clothes as well as the prize heifer he'd just bought; and the flushed winner had penned a hilarious poem in twenty rhyming stanzas about a WI shindig that went wrong when rival marmalade makers started scrapping and even ranting at the corruption of the judges, relatives by marriage, it transpired, of the unrepentant victors.

It was too close to the bone and I was sorely tempted to rise and belabour the present judges sat there smirking and jesting on the podium. Though I could hardly reasonably have fought with the winner, a stern old South Lakes practitioner in her burly mid-eighties who could have laid me on my back with a single blow. Her humorous long poem was facetious and farcical but not funny, the rhyme and metre taking lumbering precedence over all. It was like ten thousand others I'd read in the Dialect Society journal, though its extreme and literal-minded lucidity had at least one definite advantage. The London sponsor and sausage magnate definitely found it to his taste and roared spectacularly as the South Lakes comic gave it all she'd got by way of gesture, singsong enunciation and uninhibited arm-flinging.

They do things differently up in the remote sticks but even here one was not allowed to canvas the judges or seek any written commentary on one's submission. However I knew someone who drank in the same pub as the boozy retired journalist, and when after my coaching he plied him with scotch and subtly quizzed him, he was able to learn that my *Galluses Galore* had definitely arrived there safely in its Jiffy bag. Sad to say it had ruffled the feathers of all the judges apart from the journalist who genuinely believed mine was head and shoulders above the rest. I hadn't actually shaken the plumage of the London sausage man, but only because he could make neither head nor tail of it, not even the bits written in standard English.

'Head and shoulders?' I asked my friend with a small boy's intense gratitude. 'Is that what he really said?'

Yes indeed. However the rest of the judges, bar the uncomprehending Londoner, had disliked its insolent meandering and leaping about in narrative terms, not to speak of that insufferably show-off geographical jumping about: nonsensical and pointless stuff about eccentric foreigners alive and dead (Albanian braces manufacturers; Solrun's Old Icelandic Pillow Book). Worst of all though was the insistent and gratuitous political thrust; the disrespect towards decent old-fashioned patriotism and the war on behalf of the Falklands. Far too often this was aggravated by the rude, at times outrageous, language in some of the puns. All in all they really disliked the way Joe Gladstone used the dialect to do things it wasn't supposed to do; the way he focused sarcastically on national, even world events instead of restricting himself to local ones. Why spend so much time on the unfathomable and unknowable world of foreigners, when you could indulge yourself wantonly and unstintingly on Lakeland rum butter, Egremont Crab Fair, Cumberland Stew, Cumberland sausage, Kendal Mint Cake, Gilsland Show, Border TV, Bewaldeth hound trails and all the other staple dialect sources?

Sorry, edit, rephrase and rewrite that, said the journalist to my friend as he swirled and smiled at his scotch. There was something worse than the above, an even greater compositional crime that Gladstone had committed. Far too often in his story he had patronised and blithely mocked his native county and its peaceable citizens, made them out to be childlike, passive, complacent and easily led. The judges knew that Cummerlan Tyals were meant to be daft, but the daftness had to be outward and anecdotal rather than something to do with the murky inner depths of the characters involved. That combined with the disorienting outlandishness of his satire, the idiotic braces strung around the compliant lugholes had been too much for the old guard who could not place his *Galluses Galore* in any acceptable context. Two of the judges had read the first two pages and rapidly abandoned the rest. To them it felt like swotting for uphill A-levels instead of enjoying something familiar, regional and homely. It felt like highbrow slog disconcertingly mixed up and confected with the lowbrow life-affirming certainties of Bewcastle leek shows, The Biggest Liar in the World Competition, sloe gin, fox-hunting, BBC Radio Cumbria etc.

Coping with intense disappointment ought to be easier at my age but unfortunately it wasn't. It took me about a month before I could stop sulking and swearing, and get back to concentrating on my gourmet guest house and my gourmet guests. And even though I might feel well and truly devastated, Liz took it all in her stride. Apart from anything else, she said, she didn't want to stop working as an interior designer. As long as she was mobile and not gaga and they didn't take her driving licence off her, she wanted to make the most of what she was best at. As long as the ideas didn't dry up and she didn't start designing rooms and kitchens and offices in safe and accommodating and senile terms. Retirement in the sense of idleness and inanition and waiting to expire in a deck chair or on a Saga holiday was the very last thing she needed.

More importantly, in her terms she believed she owed me a lot, meaning emotional recompense, for what had started off in the dance hall with Patrick Garnett. The message of what she'd once known in a visionary context was one of purity, and her subsequent deeds as far as she was concerned had been impure and wrong and foolish. I kept reminding her that we are all allowed to err, and she said yes, but to keep on erring in old age is not the same as repetitive mistakes in youth and middle age. I said, oh, who said that, who are you quoting there, and she said, I'm not quoting anyone, it was me that said it, and that's enough. It was Liz Gladstone said it, and Liz Gladstone has also *seen* it, she has seen something that lots of people haven't, and that's what counts. Seeing is believing, isn't it, Joe?

The Author

John Murray was born in West Cumbria in 1950. He has published eight critically acclaimed novels and a collection of stories, *Pleasure*, which won the Dylan Thomas Award in 1988. *Jazz Etc.* was longlisted for the 2003 Man Booker Prize and his 2004 novel, *Murphy's Favourite Channels*, was a novel of the week in the *Daily Telegraph*. Also in 2004 Flambard reissued his 1993 satirical extravaganza *Radio Activity – A Cumbrian Tale in Five Emissions*, and in 2007 this was hailed by Adam Mars-Jones on Radio 4 as a neglected classic. In 1984 he founded the celebrated fiction magazine *Panurge*, which he and David Almond edited until 1996. He is currently Royal Literary Fellow at the University of Lancaster. He lives in Brampton, North Cumbria, and is married with one daughter.